MALE MONOLOGUES from PUBLISHED PLAYS

81 MONOLOGUES FOR TEENS & ADULTS

Edited by Debra Fendrich

MERIWETHER PUBLISHING
A division of Pioneer Drama Service, Inc.
Denver, Colorado

Meriwether Publishing
A division of Pioneer Drama Service, Inc.
PO Box 4267
Englewood, CO 80155

www.pioneerdrama.com

Editor: Debra Fendrich
Assistant Editor: Brian D. Taylor
Cover design: Mel Nethery
Text design: Lori Conary

ISBN: 978-1-56608-281-5

Library of Congress Control Number: 2022937192

1   2   3   22   23   24

Contents

* The letter in parentheses indicates the overall tone of the monologue: (C) comedic, (S) seriocomic, (D) dramatic. See Appendix A for a list of monologues by tone.

◆◆◆

Introduction

Finding the "right" monologue is usually a bit of a chore. It's rarely easy or obvious which one to select for any given project. That's typically because monologues are used for a wide variety of purposes. You might be seeking a monologue for an audition. Or maybe you are looking for a piece for competition. Perhaps you need to find a suitable monologue for an acting exercise in a theatre class.

And there are so many different types of monologues from which to choose! Some are simply an interesting narrative. Others capture a moment of raw emotion. Some call for an interesting accent or stage action that can showcase a certain skill set or strength. Of course, some are dramatic, some are comedic, and some are somewhere in between or have elements of both. Ideally, they have a beginning, middle, and end, but not always.

On top of all this, there are the vexing questions about the audience for your monologue. "What piece is most likely to sway the director?" "Should I choose something more technically challenging to impress the adjudicator or something more deep and thoughtful?" "Should I select something that will highlight my strengths?" "Will I shine the most if I perform the monologue that I like best?"

Our best advice for you is that the end determines the means in the pursuit of the "right" monologue. You almost always need to begin at the end and try to work backwards. Consider what you think the director wants or what the producers are casting for, then go find that. "But what about this...? And that...?" You're often left trying to read the mind of a stranger, leaving you to feel that the perfect monologue is impossible to find!

With this book of monologues, our aim is to minimize this frustration. We have carefully crafted it to include as many different types of monologues as possible. Our goal is to include a strong and varied collection of monologues that addresses a broad spectrum of needs so that everyone who uses this book can find the "right" monologue every time they need one.

To this end, you will find the appendices at the back of the book to be invaluable tools. A quick scan through these pages will help you quickly and easily identify the monologues that portray a character of a certain age or that are from a specific time period. Most books focus on characters of a narrow age range, almost always in the present day. Not this one! Here you will find characters as young as their early teens and as old as their 70s. Likewise, you'll find plenty of monologues that take place now, but almost as many that take place in a bygone era, whether it be decades or centuries ago. And unlike other monologue books, this collection also offers you a wide variety of running times, with some selections as short as 45 seconds and others five minutes or longer.

The table of contents and the appendices also indicate the overall tone of the monologue, whether it be comedic (C), dramatic (D), or seriocomic (S), meaning it either has elements of both or is neither remarkably funny nor delving deep into strong emotion. And you might be surprised. The tone of a particular monologue does not always align with the overall tone of the play it comes from. Rather, it's about that one character at that particular moment in the play.

No doubt, capturing the character is the most vital aspect of performing a monologue—and the most difficult. Besides the appendices, you'll find brief "About the play" and "About the scene" descriptions for every single monologue in this book to help you with the context of the piece. However, you shouldn't rely solely on these simple synopses.

To fully understand your character, it's imperative that you read the full play from which the monologue was taken. Many casting directors, adjudicators, and acting coaches absolutely insist upon only working with monologues extracted from a complete play for good reason... character. Reading the larger work helps you more deeply understand the character delivering the monologue. Knowing their arc, understanding their motivations, and having a thorough picture of their relationship to other characters all contribute significantly to help you give the best monologue performance possible.

Each and every one of these monologues is taken from a larger, published work, carefully selected from the broad collection of plays from Pioneer Drama Service. Unlike other monologue books, where it is often challenging to track down a copy of the original source of a monologue, we promise you that every one of these complete plays will always be easily attainable from Pioneer Drama Service, www.PioneerDrama.com.

Yes, ultimately this is just another monologue book. You are not going to read this book end to end and no one will, because monologue books are not really meant for that. So no... it's nothing new or fancy in that regard. But did you notice how many times we referred to this as "unlike other monologue books"? Here you'll find a wide variety of ages, of time periods, of tones, of running times... all taken from published plays that you can find easily on a single website.

Really, what sets this book apart from all those other monologue books is that it keeps you, the actor, in mind so you can find performance material here whenever you need it. We wish you all the best in your continuing journey as an actor. May the monologues in this book bring you great success, whatever your purpose may be.

The Adventures of Rikki-Tikki Tavi

Adapted by Tim Kelly

About the play: A storyteller from India weaves a tale about a wily mongoose named Rikki-Tikki-Tavi, who is the only one that can protect a British family from marauding cobras in league with Shere Khan, the arrogant tiger.

Time period: Late 1800s.

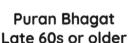

Puran Bhagat
Late 60s or older

About the scene: Puran Bhagat, an elderly holy man, makes his introduction as he offers his blessings to India, remarking on the stories that he knows and the feasts that he enjoys.

Puran Bhagat:

O, Best Beloved, I offer my blessings. For I am the holy man Puran Bhagat. I walk from one end of the jungle to the other, year in and year out, under the warming sun of Mother India. There is not a creature I do not know or who does not know me.

Ah, the stories I could tell. Wondrous stories. The rich and the poor, the strong and the weak. The good and the vile. The creatures that live on the earth and the birds that fly in the skies above. Such wondrous, magical, delightful stories— *(Sadly.)* But, alas— *(Looks into his begging bowl.)* My begging bowl is empty. See for yourself. Is it not sad? Not even the holy man Puran Bhagat, peace be upon him, can tell a good story when he is hungry. Perhaps you could spare me a morsel of something? A bit of fish, a scrap of meat. What is that tantalizing aroma? *(Sees a fish that is offered to him.)* It's a trout. A rather thin trout, but a trout nevertheless. I particularly like a trout when there's a little rice to go with it. *(Holds out the bowl as someone ladles rice into it. He then drops the fish into the bowl.)* Was there ever such a delicious meal? A million blessings be upon you. *(Hungrily eats some of the rice with his hands.)* It is a feast. A veritable feast. What's that you say? *(Listens.)* Story time? *(Annoyed.)* Can't I even finish my meal? My fish and rice. *(Resigned.)* Ah, well. What must be must be.

Alien Invasion!

By Ryan Neely

About the play: In this hysterical "War of the Worlds" parody, a regularly scheduled radio program is interrupted by news of explosions on Mars, followed by reports of objects falling to Earth in a rural California county. A Martian leader arises from the wreckage and is as clear as the stars in the sky about its plans for mass annihilation! But the courageous and determined townsfolk won't be obliterated that easily.

Time period: The present.

Bridger
50s - 60s

About the scene: Retired commando Check Bridger fires up his troops before facing the three-legged alien foes.

Bridger:

Listen up, boys! I know ya'll are just itchin' to go get you some Martian goo on your mud flaps. Let me add some fuel to the fire. I'm willing to give up my prized Gila monster boots to the first one of ya that downs a tripod! Now I know you Simi Valley boys are tough and ready to brawl the devil for a cinnamon toothpick. But you don't know tough till you know Check Bridger! I know you all's been wonderin' where I came from. So, I'll tell you a bit about myself. I raise alpacas in Apple Valley, so I know weird! I met a grizzly bear once in the woods. Them bears are tough, but Check Bridger, he's tougher. That bear mighta met me growlin' mad, but when he left, he left more scared than a cat in a roomful of dogs! There is no foolin' around here now. Tonight is gonna separate the men from the

Cub Scouts, and if you're gonna earn your badge from me, you better be able to wrestle a tiger for your stripes! Do I make myself clear?! […]

Good. Now let's go see what them Martians look like when they're inside out.

◆◆◆

Always Bella

By Kendra Thomas

About the play: The students at Lakeside High don't quite know what to make of Bella, the offbeat and somewhat annoying new girl on campus who tries so hard to fit in when she's so clearly... well, different. But Bella decides that Lakeside's star soccer forward, Katie, is her new best friend, so some classmates set out to teach Bella a lesson in humility and show her that she doesn't belong in the popular group. Once Bella's brother, Bart, helps everyone understand Bella better by sharing some sobering information about his sister's past, the students realize the dangers of judging a book by its cover and never knowing what's inside.

Time period: The present.

Bart

Teens

About the scene: After several students pull an awful prank on Bella using social media, her twin brother, Bart, tries to explain to Katie what makes Bella different and special.

Bart:

I know what you mean! But she can't help it. Bella's been like this since she was five. [...]

Before that, she was a normal kid. I mean, as normal as any five-year-old can be.

Our family was in a car accident, Katie. A really bad car accident. I was okay—just a few bruises—but Bella hit her head, hard... and our parents... well, they didn't make it. [...]

But we don't want to label what Bella has. She was injured, and now her brain works differently than most people's. She forgets things, she repeats herself, she's socially awkward... She doesn't see the world the way we do. That's the part I'm most grateful for. [...]

When people are mean to her, she finds a reason for it and moves on—quickly. She forgives them and stays her perfectly weird, bubbly self. She also has a tendency to attach herself to people. But it doesn't work out well.

At our last school, she followed this group of girls around for a while until they decided they'd had enough. They locked her in a janitor's closet. We didn't find her until late that evening. She'd been in there since noon. And now... *(Pulls his phone from his back pocket and opens up the screen, showing Katie a picture.)* ...this happened. *(Katie stares at Bart, struggling to find the words.)*

Look, I know you walked away from this, that you didn't do it. But you did let it happen... I learned a long time ago that it doesn't do any good to fight Bella's battles. But I thought if you knew a little about her, a little about her history, you might be more sympathetic.

Amelia, Once More

By David Muschell

About the play: This gripping play examines the tension between an actress and the character she portrays. Night after night, sweet Shelly Preston performs the part of wicked Amelia in an off-Broadway hit. The play's success depends on her ability to step completely and realistically into her role. Now, Shelly worries that the character is taking over her mind. She wants a night off to regain control over Amelia. However, her unsympathetic director, Alphonse Crevansky, and the ambitious supporting actress, Laura Tontelli, unite to try to convince Shelly to perform. Tom, the leading man in the play, loves Shelly and admonishes her to quit the play altogether, creating yet another force pulling on her.

Time period: The present.

Alphonse
40s or older

About the scene: We're in Shelly's dressing room, where she has just told her director, Alphonse Crevansky, that she cannot go on tonight. The director, however, has learned to court, flatter, and cajole stars into doing his bidding bidding and works to change Shelly's mind.

Alphonse:

Oh, please now, Shelly. I was certain we'd be through all these opening week flutters and done with them long ago. After all, we're entering our third month. Now, if you've called me in here to tell me you're tired, I must tell you I am tired. Everyone is tired. But we have ourselves a little hit. And to make it a bigger hit, you're going to have to work. Work makes you tired, but then you've got a hit now, don't you? And doesn't that make it all worth it? [...]

Thursday through Sunday. We come to Thursday again. Time for you to bring Amelia to life. Yes, she is excruciatingly wicked, but people seem to love watching her. You have had three days to rest. [...]

Brenda? Oh, yes, Shelly. She can do it... and I fancy I can paint like Picasso when I have a notion, but will a collector pay a Picasso price for an Alphonse Crevansky? People paid to see you as Amelia, not Brenda. *(Mocks her.)* And now you'd like to toss it all away, saying, "I'm tired! Get someone else for the show! I'm drained!" You are the attraction. *(Sweeps his hand, encompassing the world.)* They want you. [...]

(Becomes deadly serious.) A number of careers depend on you. Don't you see we have a success going? Your little self-piteous whining for a day off could lose us that. But you should know this by now!

◆◆◆

Tom
20s or older

About the scene: Tom has entered Shelly's dressing room to beg her not to just take the night off, but to leave the show altogether. He's desperate to have Shelly back and tries to convince her to walk out on the show. Unfortunately, Shelly has already transformed into cruel Amelia, making his pleas much more difficult.

Tom:

Shelly, let's quit together. Right now. No day off. This moment, right now. Let's just quit. What matters more? A few hundred people getting a couple of hours of entertainment or the happiness of someone I really care about? That's the question as I see it, and I've thought about it and decided.

The few hundred can get entertained any time, but, Shelly, I do care about you. Let's leave this mess. The show will go on without us. We can do it. We just walk out, hand in hand. I'm ready now. [...]

(Deadly serious.) Look at you. So involved in becoming Amelia that I guess you really believe you are. You're not. You're Shelly Preston pretending so hard to be Amelia that it's confusing you. You are such a dedicated actress that you've learned to lose yourself in a part. Well, this one's hurting you, Shelly. Come back. Come back out of that character. Don't leave me. [...]

I came in here a while ago and there was a confused, caring person battling with the pull of ambition, and we knew each other. I come back minutes later and I find a façade, an act. Shelly playing Amelia pretending to be Shelly. The final translation is pretty pitiful. *(Shelly is now completely in character as Amelia and tries to strike Tom. He stops her hand before it can hit him and grips her arm tightly, pulling it down to her side and holding it there. She strikes with the other hand. He counters that attack in the same manner as the first.)*

You see. What works for Amelia in a play is not as easy in real life. So many times onstage when Amelia humiliates my character, I've wanted to jump up and wrestle you to the ground and just watch the faces in the audience. You're not Amelia. Amelia lives on a stage. We're not there. I don't know what my next line is going to be. It's all spontaneous. I do know I'd like to talk to Shelly. At least to have her kick me out of her dressing room. Your life is more than a show.

◆◆◆

Bang! Bang! You're Dead

By Tim Kelly

About the play: The setting is the taping of a bizarre TV game show. The boyish host, Billy the Kid, guides two teams of contestants through a maze of facts and opinions. Prizes include such oddities as a trip to Boot Hill to view the tombstones and a coroner's pass to the next autopsy on a teenage handgun victim. The strange proceedings are stopped by a disgruntled viewer who decides the subject matter is much too serious for fun and games.

Time period: The present.

◆◆◆

Actor #3
15 years old

About the scene: An actor on the show tells Billy a story about getting a handgun and the joy it gave him, until tragedy struck.

Actor #3:

Who am I? Got up one mornin' and said to myself, "I got a fine new handgun." All mine. 'Course it was illegal, but what does that matter? I polish it and make it shine. We're friends. It makes me feel good. No one messes with me when I'm with my friend. That's what friends are for.

Only I forgot one thing. Other kids got friends, too. Colt, Springfield, Magnum, Beretta. Bang, bang, bang. I never got to see my sixteenth birthday. But I did get to see the inside of a body bag. Just like lots of my friends. *(Defiantly.)* No one messes with me. I'm tough. Or I was. I take care of business. Or I did.

(Softens.) Sometimes I wonder what being sixteen must have felt like. Who am I? I'll never know. Didn't live long enough to find out. Bang, bang, bang... Who am I?

Bayou

By Matthew Carlin

About the play: Many legends persist in the bayou, but none strikes an icy chill of fear like the mention of "Le Serpent!" Four children set out to find the creature which can supposedly take the shape of anything or anyone it chooses. The brave crew stumbles upon many creatures before they free a girl caught in a trap. She claims to live there, but no person could live that deep in the bayou. Strange things continue to happen when the children are caught by Boudreaux, the crazy hunter, and his even stranger mother. But when the rescued girl disappears, the creatures come out to help the other children escape.

Time period: The present.

Tooney
Early teens

About the scene: Tooney tells the other children a tall tale about catching a catfish so big that it snaps the motor from his boat and spits out the hook.

Tooney:

So finally I look over against the bank and there's that little tree I had done tied my trout line on... but it was bent... way down... like this! You know, kinda like Bug here looks after eatin' his mama's cookin'.

So I cut my motor and let my boat drift right up to that little tree. Well, first I figured somebody had done run right over my trout line with their boat but when I pulled on it... it was tight. Tight as a guitar string. I started to pull on it... to try to pull it up... and somethin'... pulled back. *(He changes his mood like a good ghost storyteller.)* Nearly cut my hand in two! Luckily the trout line fell across the front of the boat, which stopped it from going under... but I swear to you... when that line hit my boat it musta come within two inches of pullin' me and my old boat to a cold, watery grave!

Well, I grabbed that line with both hands and I started to pull... and pull... and pull! The farther along I got, the deeper that line seemed to go. Then... suddenly! It went limp! I leaned over into the water and up come the biggest, ugliest catfish I ever done seen! His head musta been twice the size of mine! He raised up and spit that hook outta his mouth right back at me then dove right under the boat. Why, he musta been ten foot long! He headed straight back, scrapin' the bottom of the boat as he went. He slammed right into my twenty horse Mercury! Hit that motor so hard he snapped the iron braces that was holdin' it to the back of the boat! I made a headlong dive and grabbed it just before it fell in the water! I don't mind tellin' you that motor weighs a ton, and I couldn't hold it for very long!

Well... luckily I had done run my crab nets that mornin', so I reached down' in the bottom of the boat and grabbed hold of a big one! You know those bayou crabs, they'll pinch just about anything they get close to. Well, I clamped one on one side then grabbed another, and he slapped that big ol' pincher onto the other side. Held that motor like a charm! I cranked her up and come on home!

◆◆◆

The Best Worst Day of My Life

By Dick Grunert

About the play: Student Max Griffin, geeky aspiring filmmaker, and Amanda Hughes, the most popular girl in school, are having the worst day of their lives. The school bully has stolen the only copy of Max's new screenplay, while Amanda has just been dumped and humiliated by her boyfriend in front of the entire student body. So Amanda and Max, who have never before spoken a word to each other, decide to team up and help each other in hopes of turning the atypical school day into the best worst day of their lives.

Time period: The present.

Mr. Ridge
30s - 40s

About the scene: Intense P.E. coach Mr. Ridge is tasked with giving the students proper dancing lessons.

Mr. Ridge:

All right, we've wasted enough time. Let's get started!

Now, I was going to have you climb the ropes and run speed drills today, but with the homecoming dance coming up, Principal Schumacher is making me show you numbskulls how to dance like civilized human beings. [...]

Look, I'm not thrilled about it either. If you ask me, gym class should be about two things—physical fitness and getting dodge balls thrown at your head. But sometimes we have to make compromises. Okay? Now, everybody find a partner! [...]

Let's go! You're picking a dance partner, not a new car! [...]

Okay, everybody have a partner? Good. Now, I'm going to teach you the foxtrot. We'll start with the guys. *(Leads an imaginary partner as boys try to follow.)* The basic steps are very simple—left foot forward, right foot forward, side step, touch. *(Watches as they attempt it, then shakes his head.)* Close enough. Girls, your steps are the exact opposite—right foot back, left foot back, side step, touch. Got it? [...]

Now, let's put it together and give it a try. Ready? Okay, here we go!

Bigger Than Life

By Cynthia Mercati

About the play: Tall tales, folktales, talking tales, noodles, whoppers, windies, stretchers—everyone has a different name for these stories. Whatever you call them, America's legends come to life in this play.

Time period: Early 1900s.

Pecos Bill
Mid 20s - 50s

About the scene: A cowboy asks Pecos Bill about his various legendary tales and whether they're true, including how he once rode a cyclone.

Pecos Bill:

I don't mind tellin' ya that for the first time in my life, I was a mite scared. Now you might be a-askin' yourself, just what did I do to get over it. I gave myself a talkin' to, that's what I did.

"Bill," I said, that bein' my name... "Bill, you never met nothin' yet that's got the best of you! And you're not gonna let some squint-eyed, bow legged, maggoty varmint tell you any different!" So I climbed aboard that cyclone's back. And away we went!

We were back flippin' and side windin', knockin' down mountains, blowin' holes outta the ground and tyin' rivers in knots! But in Arizona it nearly got me! It tossed and I turned! It threw me so high I had to duck to let the moon go by!

"Bill," I said, that bein' my name... "Bill, just hang on!" And sure enough, I did! I thumbed that cyclone in the withers. I flopped it across the ears with my hat just like it was my favorite hoss! And when it finally set me down, I took a look around. And dad-gummed if we hadn't cut out the Grand Canyon!

Black and Blue Friday

By Karen Jones

About the play: It's the day after Thanksgiving, and all Ellie and her new husband want is to celebrate their first holiday season at home together. But their holiday peace and quiet quickly turns into holiday chaos when they are summoned to the security office at the local mall. Seems Ellie's backwoods relatives were planning to surprise her with a visit, but first stopped to pick up some paper goods. That's when the trouble began. What they thought was a big-box store turned out to be a shopping mall full of frenzied Black Friday shoppers, and, of course, the hillbilly family ended up causing all sorts of trouble.

Time period: The present.

Bubba

Teens

About the scene: Bubba attempts to explain to mall security staff and Ellie what happened when he rode the escalator for the very first time while his brother Virgil watched, and they ended up destroying the mall's Christmas display in the process.

Bubba:

(Steps forward. Sheepishly.) I'm sorry, but I just had to try it. Them there moving stair steps. Did ya ever see such a thing? Why, if'n you can get on it, it'll do the walking fer ya.

Well, sir, while Ma and Pa and the gals went off a'hunting for their fancy Chinet plates, I decided to give those steps a whirl. Well, it looked harmless. I was just gonna ride them right down and back up ag'in. It weren't going to take me more than a couple of minutes.

Well, sir, it weren't as easy as it looked! I was being real careful like and only put one foot on to start off. But by the time that there step was actually formed, my other foot was still three or four steps behind. I kinda got drugged onto it. And there I was, 'bout split in two, a'hanging on for dear life. And then, here comes the end, and I thought to myself, "how in the world am I a'going to step off with me in that there position?"

Well, ya know, since I had that incident with the fire department last summer, they told me that for my own protection I needed to learn a little technique called the Stop, Drop, and Roll. So I did just that.

Well, it got me off 'em at least. But that little old lady and her dog didn't appreciate that maneuver very much. She weren't hurt real bad. If she had been, she wouldn't been able to whup me with her pocketbook like she did. Well, after some Good Samaritan pulled that crazy old biddy off'n me, and I finally plucked that che–waa-waa of hers off'n my boot, I started studying how to get back up those stairs without any more mishaps.

Well, I figured I had to get both feet on the same step somehow, so I jest took a running go and jumped onto those critters.

Ya see, in all that mess with the che-waa-waa, I didn't realize that my boot lace had come undone. So when I tried to jump off those things at the top, it had caught in those treads, and I come right out of that boot.

Yep, there I was sprawled out on the floor, and when I got turned around, there was my boot just a'dancing a jig on that top step. I tried to crawl back to get it, but before I could, it busted loose and came a'whizzing right at me.

I just ducked. I mean, it was a natural reflex, you know. It's a powerful big boot. Steel toe and all. But ol' Virgil here, he went for it like a bullet. You remember he was the football star back home.

You should have seen it, Ellie. Took out those reindeer in nothing flat. Looked like a bowling ball knocking down all them pins. And to beat it all, he got himself wedged under that there sleigh.

A Bowl of Soup

By Kendra Thomas

About the play: Certain foods connect us to our past, to our family, to meaningful life moments. The smell of something cooking—even something as basic as a bowl of soup—triggers memories and speaks to us in a way that nothing else can. In this soul-warming drama, five teens share what their unique bowls of soup mean to them.

Time period: The present.

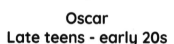

Oscar
Late teens - early 20s

About the scene: Oscar tells the story of how a pot full of tortilla soup changed his family's fortunes.

Oscar:

My dad bought an old food truck for $10,000... his life savings. "Hijo," he said, "sometimes you have to take risks!" He'd always dreamed of owning a restaurant, but he knew he'd never be able to afford it. It would take a lifetime to save up. It had taken half of one just to scrape together enough for an old food truck!

My uncle did the paint job at his body shop, and a mechanic friend fixed up the engine. I helped my dad get the old stove going and, with my sister's help, we hit the little Mexican marketplace and stocked her full of all the ingredients we would need to make the best tacos imaginable. Terlingua Tacos. He was so proud.

Our first setup was at this little food truck spot near downtown. It was like a little mobile food court. Businessmen in suits and women in high heels would walk down on their lunch breaks.

Problem was, we weren't the only tacos in town. There was a truck that had been there longer, and they weren't very happy to see us. All this guy's customers were regular and very loyal. Do you know how many tacos we sold that day? Five. Five tacos through the entire lunch rush. De nada.

The second day, we set up in a spot just a little outside of downtown. Not another food truck in sight, and we were perfectly positioned to get all the traffic from people going in and out of the courthouse. But that also meant we were perfectly positioned to get noticed by the police. Ouch. Apparently, we needed a permit. Dad didn't know. No tacos sold and a $200 fine.

We tried parks and more parking lots. Somehow Dad made just enough through the summer and fall to stay afloat... but winter? Food trucks aren't exactly at their most popular when it's freezing outside. And it was just getting bitterly cold when Dad got a permit to work a city festival. But so did a bunch of other food trucks, and we didn't have the best spot. Business was slow, and I took a break to put on my gloves and blow into my hands, trying to find some warmth. Dad threw a pot on the stove and began throwing things in it.

It seemed like he threw in a bit of everything we had and then finished it off with a touch of every spice in the truck. I was too cold to ask him what he was doing as he splashed the soup into a Styrofoam cup, sprinkled on some sliced avocado and cheese and handed it to me with a spoon. I slurped down a big spoonful... That tortilla soup was like liquid heaven on a cold day!

A moment later, a pleasant face peaked in through the truck's window. "Excuse me?" she asked, and then spied my cup of soup. Her face lit up. "What's that? I think I'll have some of that!" Dad thought fast, told her it was the day's special. Tortilla soup, $5 for a cup, $7.50 for the bigger size. He showed her the two Styrofoam cup sizes we usually used for drinks. She ordered a large, my dad made her a cup, and off she went. Two minutes later another person appeared at the window and asked for the special. Dad told me to go outside and put it on the chalkboard with the prices. Then he put another pot on the stove.

For the next three hours, we didn't sell a single taco. But we sold over two hundred cups of soup! Tortilla soup got us through the winter, and by the time summer came back around, Dad had figured out how to sell tacos, too. I love this soup. When I eat it, I think of how it changed my family's life. When I eat it, I know sometimes risks are worth it when you're chasing a dream.

The Boy Who Cried Werewolf

By Daniel Guyton

About the play: Things get wild and hairy when a group of students start to believe their teacher is a werewolf! Chris is really spooked because he's certain he saw a werewolf in his neighborhood... wearing a bowling shirt. His pals don't believe him at first, but when their teacher walks in wearing the same shirt and looking a bit worse for wear, the kids begin to suspect Chris is right! Determined to discover the truth, the young teens sneak into their teacher's home, and just as expected, the werewolf is there! Still... not all is as it seems.

Time period: The present.

Chris
Early teens

About the scene: When his classmates notice him reading a book on werewolves, Chris, an ingenious and at times reckless youth, offers a thrilling—and challenging—dark tale to inform his classmates about the werewolf that he saw last night.

Chris:

I saw one last night. I was in my room doing my homework, and I heard a dog howling, or at least I thought it was a dog. But when I looked out my window, I saw the dog standing on his hind legs! And he was wearing a bowling shirt and pants, and he had a hat on that said Nike on it. Or... maybe it was Mike? I couldn't really see it. But anyways, he looked like a man kinda, but... really hairy. Kinda like your dad, Benny, but... younger and skinnier, I think. Anyway, his clothes were ripped, and his eyes were really yellow, and he had teeth... like really long teeth. Like the way a dog's teeth look, you know, and... and then he saw me. He looked right at me, and my whole body went numb. And then he snarled, and it looked like he wanted to eat me.

I wanted to run, but I couldn't move. I just stared right at him. And that's when he howled. It was the loudest sound I have ever heard in my life, and my entire room shook. It even broke the glass on my iPad. So I ran as fast as I could down the hall into my mom's room, but my mom wasn't there. I called out to her, and that's when I heard the window break in my bedroom. So I immediately crawled under my mom's bed! I kept expecting someone to grab my leg or to bite me or to rip me to pieces! But then everything went quiet.

The noises all stopped for what seemed like forever. And that's when I heard screaming. It was my neighbor, Mrs. London. She was yelling that someone ate her cat. Yelling over and over again, "Someone ate my cat! Someone ate my cat!" It was horrible. When I finally looked out my mom's window, I saw Mrs. London standing there, yelling. But the dog, or... man, or whatever, wasn't there. But it wasn't a dog at all, you guys. It was... it was a werewolf.

The Boy with No Name
By Ev Miller

About the play: Eddy is a very special young man. Blessed with a healthy eighteen-year-old body and a winning disposition, he is also developmentally disabled, having the intellectual capacity of an eight-year-old. Kathy, his mother who wrestles with guilt over Eddy's condition, retreats into the anguished world of abusive behavior and tranquilizers. A visit by Eddy's Aunt Polly almost ignites this volatile situation into a family tragedy. There are no easy answers, but Eddy himself suggests a way to help overcome their problems and rebuild the family.

Time period: The present.

Allen
40s

About the scene: Allen, Eddy's father and Kathy's husband, is speaking with Paula, his wife's sister. She has asked him how long Kathy has been incredibly short-tempered with Eddy and unable to take care of herself because she is so drugged up on tranquillizers.

Allen:

I'm not sure. About three years ago as close as I can remember. It started about the time of my first promotion. For about six months I was out on the road a lot, sometimes for four or five nights a week. Kathy started complaining about being tied down here; that Eddy was starting to get to her. I told her I understood, that it was normal for her to feel that way under the circumstances, left alone the way they were. She took a part time job and got all wrapped up in some church work. I didn't object. I knew it was tough on her. But I thought she would snap out of it.

She was so good with Eddy when he was small. She cared for him as well as any mother could care for a child. Oh, on occasion she would make some reference to the fact that maybe we were being... *(Surprised.)* Yes, that's it... punished... for what we had done. You know, she was pregnant before we were married.

Anyway, I got promoted again, and I got in off the road a little. I started to notice a lot of things changing. Kathy started to take pills... lots of pills. She became short-tempered with everyone, but particularly with Eddy. We... we stopped seeing other couples. Kathy refused to have anyone over, and I guess they all got tired of inviting us without it being returned.

I'm sorry... you really walked into it, didn't you? I should have warned you in some way. But, Kathy was looking forward to your visit so much, and I thought it would be good for her to have you here. I still do.

◆◆◆

Eddy
18 years old

About the scene: Eddy has been speaking with his dad about school. He hopes to get paid for his after-school clean-up efforts with the teacher. When Eddy's dad asks what he would buy with the money, Eddy answers that he would buy his mother something nice, so maybe "she'd like me again."

Eddy:

How come she yells at me all the time? She never says nothing nice to me anymore.

I don't know, Dad. Mike and Greg's mom yells at them, too, but not in the same way... and sometimes she gives them hugs and kisses them... and sometimes at school when the mothers pick up their kids, even the ones in my room, the dumb ones, they kiss them and seem like they're happy to see them... Mom never smiles at me anymore. That's why I thought if I earned some money and could buy her something, she'd think I'm her boy again like she used to. 'Cuz I remember how she used to treat me. I know I can't remember as much as a lot of kids because I'm so dumb, but I remember how she used to tuck me in at night and kiss me and say she loves me and stuff. But, she don't... doesn't do that anymore.

And I remember how we all used to be so happy... all of us, like at Christmas and stuff like that. *(Swallows quickly and rushes on.)* I can remember, Dad, how I used to see you and her kissing and how warm I felt when I saw that.

Dad, how come you and Mom never kiss anymore?

The Canterbury Tales

By Burton Bumgarner

About the play: Chaucer's literary masterpiece revolutionized English literature. Tossing in a good helping of Monty Python-styled humor creates this incredibly silly yet educational comedy. You'll meet many of the pilgrims, along with a few Thanksgiving pilgrims that ended up in the wrong play!

Time period: 1300s.

Chanticleer
Ageless

About the scene: Part of the Nun's Priest's tale, Chanticleer is the greatest rooster with the most important job on the farm—waking up the whole farm in the morning. One night, he has a dream that a giant beast with big eyes came to eat him and describes it to his beloved wife-hen, Pertelote.

Chanticleer:

Oh! My dear wife! I was so afraid! I had a terrible dream! I've never experienced such a horrible nightmare in my life!

I was strutting around the barnyard, like I always do. I checked on the cow, greeted the goat, said good morning to the horse. Then, from out of nowhere came this horrible beast! He kind of looked like the dog, only he was smaller, and had very beady eyes. He looked at me like I was going to be his lunch! I tried to run toward the barn, only my legs moved in slow motion, and the beast was moving toward me faster than I could move away from him! What does it mean, dear Pertelote?

It's just scary, I mean, my Aunt Helen dreamed she heard her friend Jessica calling out for help. *(Falsetto voice.)* "You've gotta help me, Helen! I'm about to be murdered!" *(Normal voice.)* Well, Aunt Helen woke up and decided it was just a bad dream. She went back to sleep and had the same dream again. *(Falsetto voice.)* "Help me, Helen! I'm about to be murdered!" *(Normal voice.)* Aunt Helen woke up and thought it was kind of weird, but she went back to sleep anyway. And a third time she had the same dream. *(Falsetto voice.)* "Helen! Help me! Is it asking too much for a little help here?" *(Normal voice.)* This time, Aunt Helen woke up and went out in the barnyard to look for Jessica. But there was no Jessica! She was gone! All that was left was a pile of feathers! How do you explain that?

The point is, my lovely Pertelote, dreams are an important tool in unlocking the mysteries of the subconscious. Freud discovered that dreams are attempts by the subconscious to resolve conflict. Information stored in the subconscious is unruly. It cannot easily pass into the conscious, and therefore must be filtered through a censor of pre-consciousness.

Sigmund Freud, my lovely Pertelote. The father of modern psychoanalysis.

Well... the point is, I'm going to be murdered!

A Child Went Forth

By David Sawn

About the play: This beautifully written play has a powerful impact that is part emotional, part psychological, and part metaphysical. The only two characters are an old man and a young boy. They are universal types, real and familiar. The Old Man, confined to a wheelchair, reads to the boy from the works of Walt Whitman. However, lonely and ailing, he not only turns from the sentiments of Whitman, but also from the affection of the boy and any self-confrontation. The boy, understanding that the scorn of the old man is a mere cover-up for the love and dependence the man feels for him, strips the scales from the man's eyes and makes him face reality.

Time period: The present.

Boy
Late teens

About the scene: The rivalry and animosity between the old and young is an age-old archetype. Old men struggle to hold on to their dwindling power, while the young, sensing weakness, rise up in challenge. In this scathingly blunt monologue, the frustrated and angry youth lashes out at the older man, mocking the elder's physical decline and inevitable death. He fails to recognize that echoes of his own curses will someday reverberate back on him.

Boy:

You are very lonely and tired. You can't wait to die. It's funny, isn't it? How we try all the time not to think about dying. Like... it's for somebody else, right? We don't want to get old... *(Mean.)* ...like you, old man. But when we do get old and we have to wake up every morning and look at the sun, it doesn't warm us anymore. Then we want to die so quickly. But we can't. Something won't let us, and we hang on and on and on. And we get bitter, and we forget how to love.

(Puts a hand out, as if to stop the old man.) Not yet, old man! You have so many reasons to face yourself and you can't do it, can you? Can you, old man? Your hair is white and spare, your skin is wrinkled and dry, your teeth are yellow and loose, your eyesight is very bad, you drool, you can't even hear like you used to.

Remember? Remember, old man! What were you like when you were my age? Do you remember? Do you? Your skin was alive and supple, your hair was full and rich, your eyes sparkled and danced, you had strong teeth, all of those things. *(Laughs.)* Every one of them like a... a television commercial! Right? Remember? Remember what it was like to be young?

(Taunting.) Did you think then that you would be like this one day? Did you, old man? You didn't think about it at all, did you? You didn't worry about it. It couldn't happen to you, could it? But it did! And why? Why did this happen to you, and not to someone else? Isn't that the way you planned it? You kept hoping, didn't you, old man? Maybe they would come up with a new wonder drug before it happened to you, right? Maybe you could live forever! Yes! You did! Everybody does. Everybody wants to live forever! They want to get to be maybe twenty-five or thirty, then stop! Stop growing old, stop everything and just live forever. Just like that. *(Softens.)* Why can't you love anymore, old man?

Cirrius, Nebraska

By Nick Vigorito, Jr.

About the play: The town of Cirrius is so small that the mayor is also the judge and the postmaster. But the secret the townspeople hold is no small one, as a New York businessman discovers on a trip to the Brigadoon-like town. After a few meals with the locals at the bed and breakfast, the Stranger soon finds that while warm and kind, nobody can take a joke. Through a string of comically awkward interactions with the tight-lipped townsfolk, the secret behind the serious mood comes out… it is against the law to laugh. When Rose, the local school teacher, tells the Stranger about the fateful day the bizarre law went into effect, a glimmer of hope for change creeps through the gray clouds that have been hanging over Cirrius for years.

Time period: The present.

The Stranger
30s

About the scene: The Stranger is on his way to Omaha to meet up with his business partner. Making a stop along the way, he finds himself in Cirrus, Nebraska. Here, he speaks on the phone to his business partner about the strangeness of their law against laughter. He is both confused and unnerved that all the people are so nice, and yet they are not allowed to laugh.

The Stranger:

Yeah. It's me. Listen… did you ever hear of this town before I told you about it? *(Beat.)* I think they're all crazy here. I swear to God. It's against the law to laugh. *(Beat.)*

No, you heard me right, laughter is illegal here. *(Beat.)* How could I possibly make something like that up? *(Beat.)* I think you were right. No wonder it's called Cirrius. *(Beat.)* I'm not making it up! It's against the law to laugh! *(Beat.)*

I'm glad you find that funny, because if you were here now, you'd be committing a crime. I can't understand it. I can't. Because aside from this crazy law about laughing, this is the greatest place in the world to live. I'm telling you, I started thinking about maybe moving out here… to be close to the Omaha office. *(Beat.)* You'll see what I mean when you come out to the site in Omaha. I'll take you to Cirrius and show you around, maybe have breakfast with the mayor. I'll tell you one thing they are serious about, and that's their baking. They're all nuts—fresh blueberries in the muffins, fresh apples in the apple pie, tomorrow we're having cinnamon nut rolls for breakfast with the nuts that she picked from the trees out back. The nuts are nuts about nuts in this place. It's like the town of Betty Crocker with the Pillsbury Doughboy for mayor. *(Beat.)* No, I haven't lost my mind, but if I stay here much longer, I will. I'll call you tomorrow. *(Beat.)* Oh, yeah. Tomorrow night we're having steak for dinner. I probably have to help her kill the cow.

Disorder in the Court
By Brianna Dehn

About the play: Casey Licit is on a cross-country road trip when she's apprehended and held for trial in a town appropriately named Berserksville. Charged with an outrageous triple crime, Casey maintains her innocence. But as the trial begins, our level-headed defendant realizes her hapless defense attorney is an ineffective dolt, and the prosecution effectively uses silly, childish distractions to win the case, including bribing Judge Falter and witnesses with candy and leading the courtroom in the Macarena!

Time period: The present.

Scammerton
30s - 40s

About the scene: Prosecuting attorney Scammerton presents opening remarks to the jury with his unique and extremely questionable legal style.

Scammerton:

Ladies and gentlemen of the jury. What I want you to do is close your eyes with me and imagine. *(Closes his eyes.)* Now, I want you to picture a murderer. *(Describes Casey's appearance in detail.)* Imagine a girl, five-foot-three, maybe five-foot-four, depending on the shoes she's wearing. Shoulder-length hair, dark and straight, glasses, and wearing a light blue blouse with a black skirt. *(Opens his eyes.)* Now open your eyes. And doesn't that image look a lot like this woman right here? *(Dramatically points to Casey.)* Now, I would like to be known as a fair lawyer. A just lawyer. I don't want to show bias toward the things that divide us as people, things like gender. Gender is something often used to discriminate in the workplace, but not by me. I want equality across the board. Anyway, I trust that you, the jury, will make the conclusion and provide the right verdict. You all seem like an intelligent bunch. Very knowledgeable. You might say, in fact... *(Goes back to his desk to get a bucket of Smarties.)* ...that you're a bunch of Smarties. Why don't you all have some courtesy of me, the prosecution? *(Throws Smarties into audience.)* Here you guys go.

I'm inspired by great leaders—Abraham Lincoln, Martin Luther King Jr., Dwayne "The Rock" Johnson—all outstanding people who will be remembered throughout history, who have touched America. I'd like to think I also impact America, one case at a time, by keeping sickos like her... *(Points dramatically to Casey.)* ...off the street and behind bars. Does that make me a good person, a saint? The answer is yes. Yes, it does. But I still remain humble. Humble is my middle name. Actually, it's Cedric, but that's beside the point. I'm so humble, that if they held Humble Awards, I would totally win. It would be a huge affair, but I would just blow it off like it's no big deal, because that's the type of person I am. Point is, I am the good guy here, and they... *(Points to Casey and Flops, her defense attorney.)* ...they are the ones corrupting society. A vote for a guilty Casey is a vote for a safer world. Thank you. *(To Casey and Flops.)* Try and beat that.

Glen
20s - 30s

About the scene: Faulty witness and town gossip, Glen Chatter, is on the witness stand, giving the lowdown on what went down... except it's not even remotely about what went down.

Glen:

Glen Chatter, town gossip. I am the ears of the town. Nothing happens without me hearing about it. *(Looks around suspiciously and leans in.)* You want to know the lowdown? The word on the street? Well, I know this guy, who knows this guy, who knows this guy's podiatrist, and this is what I heard.

If you go to the lower eastern west side of town, and turn into the third alley you see, not the one with the dog who knows how to play the harmonica, the next one, and enter in the back of the building with no windows that vaguely reminds you of a low-budget horror movie, at the door will be a one-eyed, three-armed man named Ambiguous Pete, who will give you a very indifferent answer on whether you can enter or not.

Enter anyway, and if old Pete comes after you, ask him about his childhood. That will send him running for the hills, because confrontation is his biggest fear, right after snakes and losing a game of Monopoly.

Once you are in the building, it will give you a weird feeling, like when you see your teacher outside of school, or when you find out one of your friends is distantly related to Henry the VIII. Don't let this stop you, and you will find a woman with her fingers superglued together and bright blue eyebrows, but not above her eyes, sitting in the corner. Tell her "The geese fly south in the winter, it's time for them to come home." She will nod, and that's when you can get your Hannah Montana CDs.

◆◆◆

Dr. Evil and the Pigeons with Lasers

By Brian D. Taylor

About the play: At the monthly online meeting of the Council of Evil, the bumbling ne'er-do-well reveals his newest plans for world domination... trained pigeons... with lasers! Having heard his hair-brained schemes before, Countess Gothma, Lord Warhammer, Archduchess Arsenica, and Prince Vladi practically laugh him out of the Zoom room! Undeterred, Dr. Evil unleashes his army of pigeons upon a rainy but repellant Seattle and a harsh, brash New Jersey, only to have his plans thwarted by unexpected events.

Time period: The present.

◆◆◆

Dr. Evil
Late 20s

About the scene: Dr. Evil reveals his most recent evil plan to the Council of Evil, with not very inspiring results.

Dr. Evil:

Distinguished members of the International Council of Evil, I thank you for the opportunity to present my most recent weapon of world domination. As you all know, it has been many months since I have proposed a plan to force the citizens of Earth into submission and leave them begging for mercy. And that is because my latest plan for world domination has required the most extreme care and extra time to prepare for. But finally... after much training and careful planning, I am finally to unveil the most deadly army of minions the world has ever seen. [...]

Ladies and gentlemen of the council... I give you... laser pigeons! *(Holds up a pigeon with a tiny tinfoil hat on its head.*

Others laugh hysterically.) Hey! Stop laughing! *(They don't.)* Stop laughing! *(This only makes the others laugh more. Pounds the desk and shouts.)* Stop laughing! [...]

Thank you. As you all may know, pigeons are among the most intelligent creatures on Earth. They can be trained to complete very long journeys and find their way home immediately without error. And after a great deal of breeding and training, I have amassed the greatest army the world has ever known! [...]

I have amassed an army of hundreds of thousands of pigeons with lasers, and I have fully trained them to obey my every command. And better yet, I have created a device to be able to communicate with each and every one of them remotely, so that I—their general—may command them from afar. I'm sure you noticed my little pigeon's helmet here. *(Shows off the pigeon.)* This here is First Lieutenant Cooey, by the way. *(More laughs.)* I heard that! *(Grabs his own tinfoil hat and puts it on his head.)* With this next generation communication device, I can order my army of pigeons to destroy anything on command! And now, as a matter of demonstration, I have already sent one of my little darlings into the field to each of you so that you may see them in action. Council members, please take a look outside your windows. And say hello to my little friends! And now... watch as I command them to fire their lasers from my secret subterranean laboratory. *(Holds the tinfoil hat and begins to coo like a pigeon.)* Coo, coo-coo, cooooo!

◆◆◆

Dracula

Adapted by Stephen Hotchner

About the play: Jonathan Harker has been warned by Dr. Van Helsing, his close friend and world famous scientist, to be wary of his trip to Transylvania to close a real estate transaction with Count Dracula. But Harker is young and ambitious. He stumbles into a web of terror that nearly sends him to his death. When Harker escapes Dracula's clutches, Dracula follows him to England, knowing who his next victim will be: Lucy Wenstrom, best friend to Harker's wife, Mina. Harker and Van Helsing are unable to save Lucy from Dracula, who then turns on Mina. To break the spell, Van Helsing and Harker return to Transylvania, trying desperately to discover Dracula's whereabouts. The coach breaks down. The wolves are baying. A night of terror begins and all nearly lose lives and souls.

Time period: 1890s.

◆◆◆

Dr. Van Helsing
Mid 40s - early 60s

About the scene: Dr. Van Helsing assures Mina and Arthur, Lucy's fiancé, that it's not too late to kill Count Dracula.

Van Helsing:

No. It is not too late. Count Dracula can kill at one stroke if he desires, but he has reserved something special for Lucy. It's his revenge, Mina. Against your husband, Jonathan, and me. [...]

Hear me out and perhaps you will understand. For years, I have studied the lore of the vampire. Fact or legend, I asked myself. I studied the history of Vlad the Impaler. And when your husband, Jonathan, went to Transylvania to do business with a Count Dracula, I took him into my confidence. [...]

There was nothing I could do. Jonathan went to Transylvania to conclude a real estate transaction with the Count; an expensive estate in London. Jonathan shrugged off my warning. He felt it was merely legend... but I was concerned. If once Dracula entered England, I knew he could create a race of the undead. For Count Dracula is none other than that cruel beast, Vlad the Impaler, returning to life through some power he traded for his soul centuries ago. I fear that Lucy is falling into his power; that she, too, could become a vampire to live by night and prey on others. Come, let us take her back to the house. [...]

Carry her to the house, my brave friend. She should be herself again... at least for now.

◆◆◆

Jonathan Harker
Late 20s - early 40s

About the scene: Jonathan Harker, his wife, Mina, and Dr. Van Helsing are travelling in a coach that breaks down near Count Dracula's castle. They have no choice but to camp there until morning. As they sit around a fire with the coachman and the young women who were also passengers in the coach, Harker describes his terrifying encounters with Count Dracula.

Harker:

You must excuse Mina for leaving so abruptly, but she has her reasons. I came here last year to close a real estate deal. Dracula had purchased an estate in Purfleet, London. I ignored Dr. Van Helsing's warning not to come here. I soon discovered that the Count never meant for me to leave his castle alive. Were it not for a servant girl, Gretchen, I would be buried deep in his dungeons now... She was a very brave girl. She led me to the Count's coffin. I shall never forget the sight of him rising out of that coffin with that terrible smile on his face. I tried to kill him but failed. He escaped. Little did I know then that showing him the photograph of my wife and her best friend, Lucy Wenstrom, would spell their doom. [...]

Yes. I escaped from Dracula's castle. But in so doing turned loose the greatest menace England has ever known. Dracula came to England during a great storm. He possessed poor Lucy, killed her... and her mother. Then he terrorized the heart of London for months. Van Helsing and I tracked him down to his lair in Purfleet, but it was too late. He had left England, returned here to his castle in Transylvania, or so we believe. [...]

It was not our intention to spend the night here. This is the very worst place we could be. But that is not the most horrible part of my tale. Van Helsing and I were at Purfleet, hunting down Dracula's coffin. When we got back, we heard screams. We ran into the house, just in time to see Mina, blood running down her throat, and the Count, laughing in triumph. We stood in shock as the Count escaped. Mina lay in bed for several days. Then, two days later...

Tell them, Van Helsing. I can't go on.

The Empty Chair

By Tim Kelly

About the play: At a group counseling session for teenagers recovering from substance abuse, there's an empty chair. One of their peers, Robert, has just died of an overdose. Accident or suicide? The atmosphere is tense and uneasy. Finally, each young person speaks about their memory of Robert. The dramatic monologues tell us a great deal about each speaker and the terrors of drug abuse. Although Robert remains something of a mystery, his impact on the others is undeniable. This is a hard-hitting work with an emotionally strong anti-drug message.

Time period: The present.

◆◆◆

Speaker #5
Teens

About the scene: One of Robert's support group members, a street-wise philosopher, opens up about his complicated friendship with him.

Speaker #5:

Okay, okay, we play by the rules. *(By rote.)* My name is *[supply first name]*. I'm *[supply age]*. I'm a recovering substance abuser. I only had one friend. I only wanted one friend. I only needed one friend. Crack. You could keep your liquor and your nutritious food and your nice warm home. If I could smoke crack I had it all. I mean—ALL.

Or thought I did. I wasn't afraid of anything. Until—until—

—until Robert told me I was afraid. Boy, did I laugh at him. Then, he spelled it out for me. Like a teacher writing something on a blackboard. Said I was afraid of coming down. Said I had to keep my head twisted 'cause I couldn't stand myself when I was clean. That shook me up. Honest. Sounds simple but I never looked at it like that before. When I was smoking, everything looked different. No problems. When I wasn't smoking, I was always scared. The days when I couldn't scratch up some money were—well—I felt like I was living in hell. I felt like my skin was on fire.

Know how I got to this place? Robert brought me. He didn't stay. I turned around and he was gone. And I thought to myself, "Boy, Robert knows what it's all about. One very self-contained dude. Nothing will get him down. He'll beat the odds."

Last time I saw him he said he was joining the Marines. Didn't matter that he was underage. He had "ways."

He always talked about his folks. He made them sound like they were rich and famous and beautiful. Funny thing, though. He never seemed to go home. He was always—"around." Someplace, somewhere. I think Robert understood a lot about other people. But I'm not sure he understood himself. Maybe he didn't see enough of the world. Or—maybe, he saw too much.

Or, something like that.

◆◆◆

Fosters

By Kendra Thomas

About the play: This sweet, touching play explores the special connection between abandoned animals in need of homes and foster children who often feel alone in this world. Playwright Kendra Thomas beautifully gives everyone—human and animal—a voice to tell their story.

Time period: The present.

Petey
Older (at least in dog years)

About the scene: Petey has a reputation as a grumpy old dog who's set in his ways. And they're not wrong. But like the other characters, Petey has good reason for his skepticism. He's been hurt before—he's even missing most of one ear—and he's afraid of being hurt again.

Petey:

(Gets out of his armchair.) That's it, isn't it? People hurt you. They left Lily behind. And Mo and Tucker... no person was there for them when they needed someone. And there's thousands of others. Some dumped here, others lost and their person never came for them, and some like me.

I know I was a present. A man and a woman came and picked me out from all the other puppies—my brothers and my sisters. I think I was born on a farm. All I remember is wide open spaces... not like the streets. Anyway, they put me in a box. It was dark for a while, and I was scared. But then—the best thing—there's this light and then this kid staring down at me with the biggest smile. He named me Petey and gave me a collar with my name on it. He was the best friend a dog could hope for. We loved each other, looked after each other.

"Sometimes families don't stay together." That's what I heard the woman tell my boy one day. "Sometimes they don't stay together." She scratched my ears before she left and told me they'd come back for me. She said they'd come get me when they had a place to live. But once they left... It wasn't even a week before the man dropped me on the side of the road far away from anything I'd ever seen before. I never saw my boy again.

After that, three years on my own. I lost my ear in a fight with another dog over scraps behind a Chinese restaurant. I survived storms and freezing nights by burrowing under porches. And I learned I didn't need a person to take care of me. I don't need anyone. I don't want anyone!

At least, I think I don't... Maybe I've just lost hope that there's a person out there who needs me. *(Returns to his armchair.)*

Frankenstein

Adapted by Mark Scharf

About the play: This smart and well-crafted adaptation remains very true to Mary Shelley's classic novel. Captain Walton is on an Arctic expedition when he finds and rescues Victor Frankenstein from the harsh terrain. Frankenstein had been pursuing the Creature he created and brought to life. Having told the captain his travails before dying, it is now up to Walton to narrate the astonishing tale of the monster's creation and the resulting mayhem as the story comes alive onstage.

Time period: 1816.

Dr. Victor Frankenstein
20s - 30s

About the scene: Victor sits with his fiancée, Elizabeth. Here, he describes to her his experiment and what he has in mind for his Creature. He eloquently explains that electricity can reanimate what was once dead. Thrilled with the power of his knowledge, he does not begin to fathom the dangers he creates for both himself and Elizabeth.

Dr. Frankenstein:

(Rises and paces.) I have learned… I have seen dead bodies move—move!—have their life forces excited by a jolt of electricity. […]

My brave Elizabeth! *(Sits next to her.)* I have seen the body of a dead man sit upright when electricity was applied. […]

His muscles contracted as the life force that was left in him was excited. I know that this energy can be conveyed throughout all the nervous system, including the brain. If the tissue has not been dead too long, if there's enough of the life force left in the tissue, this energy can reanimate and control the vital forces of life. *(Rises and points out towards the audience.)*

See that burned stump of a tree there? [...]

I remember an old and beautiful oak stood there when I was young. And I remember a steam of fire and a dazzling light. [...] And when the light vanished, the oak had disappeared too, leaving behind that blasted stump. I asked my father about the nature and origin of thunder and lightning. "It's electricity," he replied. "Electricity." [...]

Man takes life away, too. So why can't man give life, restore it, as well? To examine the causes of life, we must first have recourse to death. After days and nights of incredible labor and fatigue, I succeeded in discovering the cause of generation and life. I became capable of bestowing life on lifeless matter. [...]

We change the nature of things every time we fight disease or light a candle against the darkness. We play God every time we kill an animal for food and use his skin for clothes. [...]

What about a vaccine? It was unheard of and scoffed at, and now we save lives with vaccines every day. It is our nature as man to try to make a better world for us and our children. We don't know where life truly ends and death begins. We say someone is dead, and yet hair and fingernails continue to grow. I saw a man whose brain had died, yet his heart continued to beat and his lungs continued to breathe! Listen to me, Elizabeth. We can cheat death by creating life!

Am I scaring you? [...]

(Places a finger over her lips.) Shhh. Shhh. It is all too much for you, I know. I know that better than anyone. And that is why I must pursue this for us. For everyone. How can I stand by and do nothing when I can see the way clear to help so

many? I would be guilty of a crime if I didn't. A crime against man. Believe me, you will come to see the wonder in it and be happy. [...]

I shall not let you down, Elizabeth. I will make you proud, my love. Proud.

◆◆◆

The Creature [1]
Ageless adult

About the scene: Before Victor Frankenstein died, he begged Walton to fulfill his quest to kill the creature. With the doctor lying dead nearby, Walton finds himself face to face with the Creature, who tells him of a pitiful existence. He had asked Frankenstein to create a female companion for him, but the doctor refused. That's when the Creature vowed the most hurtful revenge: to find and kill Elizabeth and then the doctor himself... his last victim.

The Creature:

Do you dream? Do you think that I was dead to agony and remorse? *(Points to Victor.)* He did not suffer in the consummation of my deeds. Oh! Not a ten-thousandth portion of the anguish that was mine. A frightful selfishness hurled me on while my heart was poisoned with remorse. Do you think the cry of my victims was music to my ears? My heart was fashioned as yours was, fashioned for love and sympathy. But I found none! And when my heart was wrenched by misery to vice and hatred, it did not endure the violence of the change without torture the likes of which you cannot even imagine!

After I murdered his brother, I pitied Frankenstein. My pity amounted to horror, but when I discovered that Victor Frankenstein, the author of my existence and my unspeakable torments, dared to hope for happiness while he left me to despair...

It was only then I was filled with envy and a bitter indignation and insatiable thirst for vengeance. I knew I was but the slave and not the master of a bitter impulse I could not disobey. Yet, when I killed his father... and when I had killed his wife... I was not miserable. I had cast off all feeling, subdued all anguish. Evil became my good. The completion of my demonic design became an insatiable passion. And now it is ended. *(Points back to Victor.)* There is my last victim!

The Creature [2]
Ageless adult

About the scene: Captain Walton, burdened by Victor Frankenstein with the responsibility to kill the Creature, remains face to face with him, while the doctor's dead body lies nearby. The Creature tells Walton of a pitiful existence. All that he wanted was acceptance and to be known as an equal to humans. Instead, he was cursed and cast aside. He knows that he is hated, but no one can hate him more than he hates himself for what he has done. Now filled with remorse, he seeks comfort in his own death.

The Creature:

Am I to be thought the only criminal when all humankind has sinned against me? Look at me. Look at me! I am nothing. I am an abomination to be spurned and kicked and trampled upon. My blood boils at this injustice! *(Turns back to Victor, ignoring Walton and his pistol.)*

Once I falsely hoped to meet with beings who, pardoning my outward form, would love me for the excellent qualities which I was capable of bringing forth. I was nourished with high thoughts of honor and devotion, but now vice has degraded me beneath the meanest animal. The fallen angel becomes a malignant devil. I am quite alone. *(Faces Walton.)*

Do not be afraid. I will cause no more harm. You hate me, but not as much as I hate myself. I shall leave your ship on the ice raft that brought me to it, and I will seek the most northern extremity. There I shall build my funeral pyre and consume to ashes this miserable frame. I will die. I will no longer feel the agonies that now consume me or feel those passions and desires I can never quench. He who made me is dead, and when I have joined him, the memory of us both will quickly vanish. Polluted by crimes and torn by bitter remorse, where can I find my rest but in death?

Gossip

By Brian Hampton

About the play: Gossip is personified as a charming yet sinister new student befriended by a group of high school students. She immediately makes herself right at home as the new "Queen Bee," secretly manipulating and twisting the truth to get what she wants. But as her new friends begin to figure it all out, they turn on her as ruthlessly as she went after them, leading to a surprisingly twisted ending.

Time period: The present.

Andy
Teens

About the scene: This monologue comes toward the end of the play, after all of Gossip's games have played out and her so-called "friends" have figured out her end game. One of the students, Andy, narrates how they had begun to turn on Gossip, one by one, standing up for themselves again. He describes Gossip's last days in school and what happened after she left.

Andy:

It was as if her voice didn't exist anymore. It was as if she didn't exist anymore. People stopped listening to her ideas, her complaints. They began to stand up to her. Ignore her. When she would come into a room, people would scatter. She was depressed. She was left with no one. She showed up for the auditions for the musical, but she bombed it. She couldn't hit any of the notes she had hit before. Her acting was terrible. And she blamed everyone else. [...]

The day the cast list was posted was the last day any of us saw her. Then, two weeks into rehearsals, we were all called into a special assembly. We all thought it was one of those guest speakers or something about the dates of finals, but as we all sat in the dark, the principal came out. There were three therapists present on the stage, too. They were there not to talk to us about school, but to talk about death. Gossip had died. Tim took it hard. So did Dallas and Kaine and Candy. But no one as hard as me. I had seen it all and, even though we once thought she deserved losing all her friends, we knew we had made a horrible mistake. We should have told her why we stopped talking to her. We showed her no compassion. We were as ruthless as her. Everyone had "kick me" signs on their backs, but instead of being honest with her, we all put our signs on her back. There was a moment of silence the next day at the school. But when the funeral came, I was the only one who decided to go. Something didn't seem right. I don't know why. Something just told me to go.

The Great Gatsby

Adapted by Gary Peterson

About the play: A self-made millionaire, Jay Gatsby's desire for wealth, popularity, and power in the Jazz Age hides a deeper passion—his love for Daisy, the woman he met and fell for years ago, but who has since married wealthy, hulking browbeater Tom Buchanan. When Daisy's cousin, Nick Carraway, happens to become Gatsby's unwitting neighbor, he soon finds himself to be a liaison between Gatsby and Daisy. Nick narrates this tragic story of thwarted love, exposing how wealth, materialism, and decaying moral values corrupted the American dream amidst the opulence and dance parties of the 1920s.

Time period: 1922.

Nick Carraway
30 years old

About the scene: Nick's iconic opening monologue to the audience introduces his neighbor, the mysterious Jay Gatsby, who is dimly lit with his back to the audience.

Nick:

In my younger and more vulnerable years, my father gave me some advice that I've been turning over in my mind ever since. "Whenever you feel like criticizing anyone," he told me, "just remember that all the people in this world haven't had the advantages that you've had." He didn't say any more, but we've always been unusually communicative in a reserved way.

(Gestures to Gatsby.) That's not me. That's my neighbor, millionaire Jay Gatsby, and that's how I first saw him that hot summer in 1922, standing there alone one night, staring across the estuary from West Egg, New York over to the more

fashionable town of East Egg. *(Points to the green light.)* That's where the real money lives—East Egg. Don't get me wrong, my family did fine. My family have been prominent, well-to-do Midwesterners for three generations. The Carraways are something of a clan, and we always tell people that we're descended from the Duke of Buccleuch, whoever he was.

The actual founder of my family line in America was my grandfather's brother, who came here in 1851. He was rich and canny enough to pay the $300 to have someone else fight in his place during the Civil War. Instead of fighting, he started a wholesale hardware business that my father carries on today. But ours is new money. This is generally an object of scorn by the old, landed wealth you'll find there across the water. Theirs is the world of polo ponies and idle, languid afternoons in bright sunshine.

That's where my cousin lives. Well, second cousin, really, once removed. Daisy Buchanan and husband Tom. I hadn't seen her in years. Tom I knew somewhat from Yale, where we both went to college. Still, I was invited to their palatial home one afternoon for dinner and drinks. *(Scoffs.)* Booze, during Prohibition. Liquor is illegal in the United States, but the gentry always has it flowing anyway. Welcome to the world of affluence and privilege in the Roaring Twenties.

Jay Gatsby [1]
32 years old

About the scene: Gatsby takes Nick into the city to inform him of the plan to meet Daisy. On the way, Gatsby explains more of his background so Nick doesn't get any wrong ideas about him.

Gatsby:

How do you like my car? [...]

I can go faster. I never get a ticket. I did a favor for the police commissioner once. Look here, old sport, what's your opinion of me anyhow? [...]

Well, I'm going to tell you something about my life. I don't want you to get a wrong idea of me from all these stories you hear. *(In a rehearsed manner that suggests he's told the story before.)* I am the son of some wealthy people in the middle-west. They're all dead now. I was brought up in America but educated at Oxford because all my ancestors have been educated there for many years. It is a family tradition. [...]

My family all died, and I came into a good deal of money. After that I lived like a young rajah in all the capitals of Europe— Paris, Venice, Rome—collecting jewels, hunting big game, painting a little, and trying to forget something very sad that had happened to me long ago. *(Nick starts to look incredulous.)*

Then came the war, old sport. I accepted a commission as first lieutenant. In the Argonne Forest, I took two machine-gun detachments so far forward that there was a half-mile gap on either side of us where the infantry couldn't advance. We ended up ambushing three German divisions. I was promoted to be a major, and every Allied government gave me a decoration— even Montenegro. Little Montenegro down on the Adriatic Sea! *(Takes a large medal on a ribbon from his pocket and hands it to Nick.)* That's the one from Montenegro. Turn it over. [...]

(Takes a photo from another pocket and hands it to Nick.) Here's a photograph of me and my chums from my Oxford days. I'm

the one with the cricket bat. The man on my left is now the Earl of Dorcaster. [...]

I told you it's me. I'm the one with the cricket bat.

Look, old sport, I'm going to make a big request of you today. I thought you ought to know something about me. I didn't want you to think I was just some nobody.

◆◆◆

Jay Gatsby [2]
32 years old

About the scene: Gatsby describes to Nick the events of the car crash he and Daisy were in earlier in the day and his realization that spending his life with Daisy was just a dream that would never come true.

Gatsby:

Daisy was driving when... [...]

I think my reactions would've been quicker. I could've avoided the accident.

She was at first frozen at the wheel. She drove miles before we finally stopped. Then it was like it all hit her at once, and she was pretty shaken up. I finished the drive home. I watched her house for a while, made sure Tom wasn't going to bother her after that unpleasantness of the afternoon. She locked herself in her room and if he tried any brutality, she was going to turn the light out and on again to signal me. But once I saw she went to bed, I came back here. *(Pause.)* I hid the car in my garage. [...]

I'll tell everyone I was the driver. I can take the heat. [...]

(Sighs heavily.) She's going to stay with Tom, you know. [...]

I knew it the second Tom mentioned their daughter. That is a bond that could never be broken. Certainly not... certainly not by a fellow like me.

(Reflectively.) Do you know that when Daisy and I were dating, I always wore my uniform? This was totally accepted. People showed respect to an Army officer during the war. But the real reason I did it? I was so dirt poor that I didn't own any civilian clothes. Don't know whether Daisy knew that. Her world was so different, Nick. Her family was so rich. I'd never seen any house like the mansion she lived in. When I came back from overseas, I wanted so much to be in with that crowd. To show her I was worthy of her. And here she was with this... this polo player.

I had chased after a dream—no, it was the memory of a dream. One fleeting moment in time that could never be recaptured.

If These Walls Could Talk

By Robert Swift

About the play: This insightful play confronts the problems of today's youth with honesty and forcefulness. Elaine, now a successful author of a self-help book, returns to high school five years after graduation to receive an award. Through her memories, we meet a fascinating gallery of recognizable young characters. The timeless issues of high school students are addressed head-on while retaining an upbeat and positive outlook.

Time period: The present.

Stanley
Teens

About the scene: Stanley explains his attachment to his varsity jacket to Rose Marie. He is quite attached to his varsity jacket— so much so that he won't go to prom because he would have to take it off to wear a tux. After being called out on his juvenile attachment to this piece of clothing, Stanley starts to wonder if maybe he is being too ridiculous.

Stanley:

I could never go anywhere out of my varsity jacket.

Have you ever seen me without my varsity jacket? This varsity jacket is like my flesh. You wouldn't expect a guy to walk around without his flesh, would you? That would be grotesque.

I can't imagine life without my varsity jacket. My life, anyway. See, I used to be nothing special. No Kid Zero, but nothing special. I even heard some kids say that about me one time. "That Stanley Brown—he's nothing special." I don't have much academic smarts. I know that. I guess I don't have much ambition, either. Maybe that comes later.

I do know my life turned around when I got my varsity jacket. People even looked at me different. Y'know—I was one guy who'd achieved something. I was somebody. Out of the ordinary. Special. I tell you that feeling was GR-R-R-E-A-T. It still is. I know some kids might think it's definitely bizarro. But it's my life, isn't it? Truth is, I can't give up wearing my varsity jacket, because, well—I'm scared.

I don't want to go back to the way it was. I don't want to be— "nothing special" again.

In the Hood

By Pat Lydersen

About the play: The corner of 159th Street and 43rd Avenue is a lively neighborhood. Kids play hopscotch while the shop owners take care of their businesses. But kind, old Mr. Fineburg is in money trouble and about to lose all the buildings he owns thanks to Mr. Guy Jantic. The greedy businessman is threatening to purchase the properties and turn the street into a state-of-the-art parking lot. Mr. Fineburg's tenants, who are also his friends, get together with other residents to try to save their "hood." It looks like they're doomed to failure until modern social media saves the day.

Time period: The present.

Guy Jantic
40s or older

About the scene: Because Mr. Fineburg has failed to pay his property taxes, his buildings are up for auction, and the greedy business typhoon Guy Jantic currently has the highest bid. Jantic plans to evict all the tenants, tear down the buildings, and build a parking garage. As Jantic shares his plan with the residents of the neighborhood, he responds to one of the kids who yells out that they don't need a parking lot.

Guy Jantic:

Don't need a parking lot? My boy, how little you know! How naïve you are! This so-called neighborhood of yours is a throwback to the old days. It needs to be torn down to make room for the future. You're in a city now, my friends. There's no room for neighborhoods. Look at all those shiny new office buildings down the street with workers hurrying around with their briefcases in hand. *(Indicates a different direction.)* Look at the immense department stores with people coming and going, their bags filled with the latest gadgets and fashions. We are in an exciting city, my friends, a hustling, bustling, exciting city. It's wonderful, wonderful!

There is one fly in the ointment, though. One problem which all cities must face. It's a terrible, terrible problem, which only men such as I, Guy Jantic, can solve. That problem, my friends, is parking.

Ah, but you're just a child. You have no understanding of how the world works. The need to find a parking place when there is none to be had is the most frustrating endeavor a man can face. It can turn normally pleasant individuals into raging beasts! It can, in truth, tear apart the very fabric of our society! But I, Guy Jantic, shall not let that happen. I, Guy Jantic, shall solve this terrible problem. I shall build a multi-level garage to house thousands of cars! It will have elevators, ramps, signs, and spaces painted in lovely yellow lines! People will come from miles around to park in my garage. They will pay going in, they will pay going out, and all that money will be mine!

Jim Bridger—Mountain Man
By Willard Simms

About the play: This show covers fifty years in the life of Jim Bridger, one of the earliest mountain men in the expanding United States and the trailblazer who trained Kit Carson as a guide and scout. Bridger recounts his "tall tales," speaks out against the injustice done to Native Americans, and mourns the encroachment of civilization.

Time period: 1860s.

Jim Bridger
60s

About the scene: Bridger talks to the ghost of Daniel Boone about the modernization of society.

Jim Bridger:

I'd rather look death square in the face than you, Dan'l. Death ain't particular, but you, there's only a few of us you'll come after. A few of us you'll judge. *(Rushes to the ghost.)* Whoooo-eee, I did me a job out here, didn't I?!! Goddammit, I did! Too good a job. God knows I worked hard in my life, but it don't look like I'm gonna enjoy the fruits of my labors none. Fruit spoiled and went bad. Yeah, I know if I hadn't opened things up it would'a been somebody else. But later, Dan'l, a lot later.

Oh, I had me some dreams when I come out here. God almighty I had me some dreams! The few that come true, it weren't never like I figured. What mattered most was the doin', 'steada how it turned out afterwards. Wish I'd have known that then. God, how I loved the doin'! Long as I was workin' I was happy. I knew I was part of the air I was breathin' and the ground I was workin' on. But that work ain't yours no more, once it's finished. So don't judge me too harsh. These times now... I'm like a oak tree growin' up in an apple orchard. I don't fit, I need too much room, and I don't take to tender, lovin' care.

I been all over and it's always the same. Folks worshippin' progress like it was a God; everythin's gettin' better'n better. They're afraid of the wilderness, and they're afraid of the men that understood it. They already got most of the Injuns put away in outdoor jails. Plains are turnin' into dust, the forests are gettin' cut back. And it's always a group of men makin' the decisions, so you can't stick the blame on no one person.

I done some things to be ashamed of. Once I left a friend to die. Left him alone, out in the wilderness, nobody around for miles but hostile Injuns. I was nineteen, me and another feller was left behind to bury him when the time come for it. Oh, he was in bad shape. A bear'd busted him up and half tore his head off. Couldn't even recognize him, and he was smelling something terrible. We stayed four days and then lit out. I been tryin' to make up for that my whole life. Well, he was bound to die, but he was takin' so long! Injuns would have found us and... and he didn't die. He spent twenty days crawlin' through the brush, his hatred for me the only thing 'keepin' him goin'. Eatin' snakes and berries and torturing me in his head. Finally went out of his mind from the pain, but he kept goin'. Got found too, so disfigured nobody knew who he was and rantin' and ravin' about men bein' worse animals than bears. He was... he was never a man again, been better for him if we'd of shot him. It was me... done that to him. But I know it and I carry that scar!

Scars ain't fashionable no more. You organize things, hide behind a system, and don't feel nothin'. You're dealin' with rules or ideas or projects... never with people. Folks workin' for a company, and it's always the company decides things, not them; somethin' goes wrong, it was the others talked you into it. Back in your time there was always a frontier to find yourself in. What's it like where you are now, Dan'l? We ought to explore it together. I'll bet there's many a trail needin' to be blazed. I've fought Injuns just like you, killed a bear with a knife singlehanded, just like you. But how do you kill progress? There was a time when one man made a difference out here, when he could have the whole territory in his back pocket. Men like us, we're lookin' for freedom, Dan'l, it's mother's milk. We live off it and we live for it. A bird in a cage, he ain't free in that cage, but he's safe, he gets taken care of. The country's turnin' into a cage, Dan'l, what am I gonna do?!

Dan'l, come back!!! Don't leave me like Beckwourth and Fitzpatrick. Don't go! Don't go!

The Last Leaf

Adapted by Thomas Hischak

About the play: This bittersweet O. Henry adaptation involves Johnsy, a young artist, who lives with her friend Sue in an artists' colony in Greenwich Village, New York City. Among the other artists who reside there is a frustrated artist, Old Behrman, who has unsuccessfully been trying to make a living as an artist for forty years. Johnsy is suffering from a severe case of pneumonia and has lost her will to live, telling Sue on a blustery November day that she will die when the last leaf falls off the vine she sees out the window from her sickbed.

Time period: 1907.

◆◆◆

Old Behrman
73 years old

About the scene: For 25 years, Old Behrman has been trying to paint a masterpiece. Frustrated at his lack of success as an artist, he seldom paints anymore though he still cares greatly about art and his artist neighbors in the colony. Old Behrman is alone in his apartment but has left the door open to see when Sue returns from the market.

Old Behrman:

(To canvas.) Just look at you. Stubborn, so stubborn to keep me waiting so many years. *(To audience.)* But she will come. My masterpiece. *(To self.)* But it is too cold today. In all the years since I first came to the colony, never can I remember such a cold November. It is ... how many years, now? *(To audience.)* Too long. When I came to this Greenwich Village I says to myself, Behrman, this is the place for the artist to live. They must have heard Old Behrman, for over the years, everybody comes. Cheap rents, poor artists, little rooms, friendly people.

Soon it is called a colony. That I like. *(To canvas.)* So for how many years, you and me, we live in this colony? *(To self.)* Silent and stubborn. Such a beauty...

(To Sue, who has entered the hallway area, wrapped in a cloak and carrying a small bag of groceries.) Ah, Sue! You are there! You bring medicine for your friend, no? I do not believe in medicine. For seventy-three years, no medicine is good for me. [...]

The two of you next door... I hear you and your feet noise and I think: what can two such young people do alone in this world? Two artists, yes; and two friends. But so young, each of them. [...]

Poor Miss Johnsy. Mr. Pneumonia is not so nice to pick on such a one like she. Why not he try to fight Old Behrman? I'll show who is afraid of him!

Legend of Sleepy Hollow

Adapted by Vera Morris

About the play: Ichabod Crane, a lightly goofy schoolmaster, comes to the farming community of Sleepy Hollow with all his worldly possessions. He's looking for a good life and a wealthy wife who will supply it. Once he sets eyes on the local beauty, Katrina Van Tassel, he's sure his dream will come true. Unhappily for Ichabod, Katrina has a boyfriend who's extremely jealous... the boisterous Brom Bones. He knows the superstitious Ichabod believes the graveyard to be haunted by a small army of restless spirits, including the most famous phantom of all, the Headless Horseman, and he uses that to his advantage.

Time period: Early 1800s.

Brom Bones
20s

About the scene: Brom Bones claims to have just encountered the Headless Horseman while riding his horse, Daredevil. He dramatically bursts into the town dance to tell his frightening tale to the superstitious townspeople.

Brom Bones:

(Mysterious.) I barely escaped with my life. [...]

If you call the Headless Horseman mischief, then I guess I was up to mischief. [...]

I not only saw him, I met him. *(Slow, scary tone.)* I was riding back from Tappen Zee. I knew I was late for the party, so I nudged Daredevil and he started to gallop. He could smell the storm coming and his nostrils went wide. But it wasn't the storm he was smelling. It was the Headless Horseman. There he was right in front of me... huge, misshapen, towering. He offered to race me for a cup of punch. [...]

He had a head alright. It was stuck on the pommel of his saddle. [...]

I would have won the race. Daredevil was sure to beat the goblin horse. But as we came to the church bridge, the Hessian bolted and vanished in a flash of light. I'm lucky to be alive.

Little Women
Adapted by Gary Peterson

About the play: This fine adaptation of the literary classic by Louisa May Alcott is rich with strong and superb acting roles for all performers. Four sisters, each with a distinctively different personality, offer an irresistible charm as we see them grow up to experience life's joys and disappointments.

Time period: 1860s.

Laurie
20s - 30s

About the scene: Neighbor Laurie has just arrived back to the March home after spending some time in Paris. Quite unexpectedly to Jo, he is now married to her sister Amy. Jo and Laurie were nearly wed when they were younger, but she cut off their courtship, insisted they were not a match. Here, Laurie explains to Jo the turn of events that led to his and Amy's seemingly hasty marriage, and how they are in fact a perfect match, never having known it in childhood.

Laurie:

Well, we got your letter, and we all made plans to come back to America. Grandpa, your aunt, me, and Amy. But your aunt had some prudish notion about chaperones and such nonsense, and just wouldn't let Amy come with us. That delayed everything. Finally, I just settled the difficulty by saying, "Let's be married, and then we can do as we like." [...]

It actually wasn't so great a step as you might think. You know, Amy and I had been seeing quite a lot of each other in Paris, and we became very close. Closer I think, than we were in the old days here in this armchair. She really is quite wonderful.

Do you want to know the day I knew? I mean, the day I knew she really was the one for me? I can tell you. It's a small thing, but I know you will understand.

On summer days, we used to go out boating. But my arms would get tired rowing out there to the middle of the lake. Amy could see I was tired of the rowing, all by myself, with her sitting there with her parasol. So she says, "Why don't you give me one of the oars, and we can pull together?" Pull together. It was so simple and so cooperative a solution that I saw in an instant what a good wife she would make. Oh, she's a rotten rower. Don't tell her I said so. She uses both arms, and she pulls all wrong. We'd have gone all in circles if she rowed by herself. But that's not the point. We rowed well together. It was great fun, and neither of us were tired.

My wife is quite sweet, Jo.

Professor Bhaer
Late 30s - early 40s

About the scene: While at boarding school in New York to work on her writing, Jo meets Professor Bhaer, who teaches German and English to his students. He is very invested in Jo's writing and eventually helps her publish her first book. Here, he is disappointed in a short story she has written for a publication. He sees more potential when she speaks about the things she holds near and dear to her heart and encourages her to delve into more personal topics when writing.

Professor Bhaer:

(Disappointed.) It's a very exciting and imaginative story, Jo. [...]

Yes, but. *(Sighs.)* But, you are capable of much more. Just now, when I asked you to describe your sister, what did you do?

I'll tell you what you did. You spoke at length about her various good points and bad points. You said she is a mixture of traits. This is because she is a real person. Real people are very complex. Here, we look at your villain in "The Maroon Heart."

How is he described, your villain? He is described as a villain. *(Reads.)* "Black-hearted Peter was a villain who always preyed on the innocent by night." This is not a character. This is a caricature. He is a villain. You say so, and no one will expect any more from him. But real, genuine people are far more complicated than that. Consider Hamlet, Juliet, Ivanhoe. These great, timeless characters are riddled with character flaws, *(Pointedly.)* and that's what makes them interesting.

You have seen the stories I write, yes? Humorous little funny stories. Nothing of much consequence. But what do I wish I could write? Do you know Schubert's lieder?

Each song has a tone that transcends mere language. Franz Schubert has been dead for forty years now, and yet his songs are alive. That is what I wish I could write. The words of a Goethe, a Müller, or a Sir Walter Scott, set to a music that goes straight to your heart.

Now, I can see this great writing—this stirring music. I recognize its greatness, but I cannot write it. I have not that singular gift. But you do, Jo. I have seen this in the other writings you have shown me. I hear it when you describe the people you love. You could write a story that will not just be read in this week's edition of "The Volcano," but one that will be read and enjoyed by people a hundred years from now.

For they will still have hearts, and you will touch them.

(Seeing Jo saddened.) Ach, here I am, the literature professor again! Don't look so downcast! It is quite an accomplishment to get anything published. You made money, yes? You can pay the bills! You can eat!

Stick to it, Jo. You have a talent. Do not waste it on trifles. You could do something great. You could have a book on the same shelf as Shakespeare.

Love at First Thought

By Shawn Deal

About the play: Norm has a quirky habit of sharing his favorite books by leaving them for someone else to find and hopefully treasure. When he watches a girl he's gone to school with for years, Jolaine, discover his favorite Shakespeare play he left on a park bench, they share a look and a smile that creates a magical moment of connection. Both Norm and Jolaine are with their best friends, providing the audience four different points of view on this burgeoning relationship. These perspectives are cleverly revealed through internal monologues during which the four characters speak their inner thoughts out loud.

Time period: The present.

◆◆◆

Norm [1]
Late teens - early 20s

About the scene: Norm and Jolaine have just shared a look and a smile. As the other characters freeze onstage, Norm gets lost in an internal monologue about their moment of connection.

Norm:

The look she just gave me... That was the strangest thing to ever happen to me. I mean, maybe not strange... No, that's what I mean... but in a really good way. Granted, if I had ever seen a UFO, well... that would have been the strangest thing. Or if I had ever seen Bigfoot stomping around in my backyard... certainly that would have been stranger. But up until this moment right now in my life... that was the strangest thing to ever occur.

Maybe I need a more exciting life? *(Shakes his head, then gets excited.)* Nah! How much more exciting can it get than what just happened? I just got a girl to smile at me! Whoo! Whoo!

High-five! *(Runs around trying to get a high-five from John, who is frozen or in the dark. Realizes he's deep in his own thoughts.)* Okay. High-five just me, then. *(Slaps his own hand, then comes to a revelation.)* I clearly have to talk to more girls! What makes this moment so strange is that I felt a connection there. For whatever reason, our eyes met, there was this moment—we looked at each other in a way we haven't ever before... For a brief, quick moment there, we had something—we both shared something in that look. I have no idea what that something was—or is. I don't know if it was something metaphysical, spiritual, supernatural, some sort of hocus-pocus, or just something very simple. I made her smile and her smile made me smile.

◆◆◆

Norm [2]
Late teens - early 20s

About the scene: Norm finds himself tongue-tied as Jolaine thanks him for sharing his favorite Shakespeare play with her.

Norm:

(To Jolaine.) Yeah... no problem... whatsoever...

(Looks at Jolaine and starts to panic a bit. To himself.) I am failing under the weight of grand expectations. I just gave a girl a play by William Shakespeare. The greatest wordsmith in the entire history of... history! There is no way I am coming up with a word, a string of words, or a paragraph that will come anywhere close to any single phrase the Bard ever put on parchment. What do I say to a girl that Shakespeare hasn't already said better? He invented something like 1,500 new words—and they were all cool. If I invent a new word and tell her, I'm going to look insane! And I do have to worry a little bit

about what Shakespeare has told me about love. He's told me that love is an instant sensation that sweeps over you like a... tsunami wave. You fall hard, head over heels in love. Which, if true, sounds like I would break half the bones in my body. And there is the whole death thing if you can't be with them, or your friends don't like them, or you have to keep it a secret... That seems too extreme for me.

(To Jolaine.) Umm... let me know when you finish it... and... you know... you can... tell me if you liked it—or not liked it— or whatever...

Lover's Leap

By Tom Gillespie

About the play: Janet is at the top of Lovers' Leap on a moonlit night, contemplating jumping. Her actions are interrupted by an array of characters including an eager newspaper reporter looking for a big story. No one cares to try to stop her until Dick arrives to show her that life can be beautiful if two "invisible" people will only notice each other.

Time period: Late 1970s.

Reporter
Late 40s - 50s

About the scene: As Janet ponders jumping off the cliff, the reporter is there to capture the moment with his camera and tells Janet how he sees the story—her story—unfolding for him.

Reporter:

That's the "before" shot in a prizewinning... keep my fingers crossed... before and after series. Know what I mean? Why the hell did Life have to fold?! *(Janet continues to stare.)* Tasteful, of course. Not too much gore in the "after" shot... uh, down below. Restrained. You don't want to beat people over the head with it, ruin their breakfast. Know what I mean? Next, we get one just as you *(Makes diving motion with hand.)* go over the edge... if, *if* you're gonna do it?

I don't want to rush you, or anything, but it seems to me this is the sort of thing... well, you'd want to get over with in a hurry. I would. Like getting into a cold swimming pool. I just walk right up and dive right in. *(Janet just looks at him.)*

Well, different strokes for different folks, as they say. But I got this brilliant idea for a picture feature. So I'd been waiting up here for a couple of hours and was about to pack it in when you came along and I said to myself, this may be my lucky night after all. Know what I mean? *(No response.)* But you've just been standing there dithering for a long time... writing... thinking... writing. What is it? A farewell note? Not real talky, are you? But maybe I got it all wrong. Maybe I've just been wasting my time? Listen, tell me... are you planning to...? *(Makes diving gesture with hand. Janet nods "yes", though a bit doubtfully.)*

Good... no, wait... I don't mean that the way it sounds. It's just that if you're gonna do it, what do you care if I get a shot of it? Right? No skin off your nose. Us reporters are a pretty cynical lot. Know what I mean? We get that way from seeing life from the sad and seamy underside, plus from watching movies like "The Front Page." Did you see it? You ought to. But underneath our sardonic veneer, we got hearts of gold. Reporters and prostitutes. What's your name, by the way? *(No reply.)* Know why I came up here tonight? Why I figured there'd be a leaper? Because there's a full moon. *(Points.)* Look at that. Beautiful, huh? That means more people are gonna knock themselves off tonight. It's a proven scientific fact. Isn't science marvelous? Did you know that suicide is on the upswing? Up 20 percent over last year. And the age is getting lower... more young punks opting out, as they call it. Say, how old are you, by the way? About 28? 29? [...]

Hey, I got an idea. Want me to print your last message? Let the world know why you done it? *(She shakes her head.)* Don't be like that. Give me a quote. How do you feel about things as you contemplate self- destruction? What thoughts are passing through your head as the last minutes tick away before you do the final and irrevocable deed? What advice have you got for other miserable souls in torment? What's your opinion of Women's Lib? What the hell do you gals want, anyway? What bitter dregs did life deal you off the bottom of the deck to lead you down the garden path to this fateful point in time? Listen, young lady, I suppose you think I'm hard and unfeeling. Let me tell you my side of it. *(With feeling. Bitter.)* I'm about to lose my job. It's on the line. I gotta show 'em I still got plenty left on the ball. All these smart-ass kids fresh from J school... they all think they're... what's their names?... you know... Redford and Hoffstein? This is the sort of feature the wire services might pick up. Give my career a lift. I'll show the little punks. Girlie, I'm talking about my livelihood. Look, I *worked* on this idea. I did research. *(Recites rapidly, mechanically.)* Japan is number one suicide-wise, Sweden next; the US of A is closing fast; New Jersey leads all the states and no wonder; most attempts are at night, during a full moon; guns are the most popular method... *(Janet looks pained, raises a hand in protest.)* Well, I thought you'd be interested, under the cir-cumstances. Why not do me a good turn as your last act on earth? What'll it cost you? Live and let live. You think it's easy being a reporter for a two-bit newspaper? You think it's a decent living? You think you got troubles. I could tell you things that would make you cry your little eyes out. You kids think you're the only ones with problems. Ever consider what it's like for a guy my age to get a better job? Spend a lifetime in the rat-race and whattaya got to show for it? Bills, alimony, a mortgage, an ulcer. God! Move over, baby. *(An idea.)* Hey, you got pretty good legs. Sit up there on that railing. *(Raises camera.)* I know some photogs would caption it, "Just Before the Cheesecake Fell." I'm not that bad... *(Chuckles.)* It's kind of funny at that. *(Janet sighs, continues to write.)* I don't know why you're acting like this.

The public has a right... a need to know. You may have heard of the first amendment? Freedom of the press? What do you think the Bicentennial was all about? [...]

What the hell kind of letter you writing, anyway? Say, do me a favor... I'm starving. You don't seem to be in any rush to... *(Makes the over-the-side gesture.)* Let me go down to the bottom for a sandwich and cup of coffee. Boy, is coffee murder on my ulcer, but what are ya gonna do? I've gotta get something on my stomach. Hold off 'til I get back? Huh? Will you? *(Janet sighs, shrugs, nods slightly.)* Promise? I'll be right back. I can't go unless you promise. [...]

I appreciate it. You won't regret it. When I write you up, you'll be a gorgeous blonde. [...]

(Magnanimously.) So who'll know? You may have noticed in news stories all females between 16 and 60 are blonde, big-busted, and beautiful... if they died violently. Of course, murder's best... but what the hell. Don't go away.

May I Have Your Attention, Please?

By Catherine Rhoden-Goguen

About the play: The Borthwick family gathers in the living room after being asked to convene there by the self-appointed black sheep of the family, Chris. He, however, has not shown up, and the family is none-too-eager to take time away from their busy schedules. Chris finally arrives via video and speaks to them from the television screen. We begin to see his perspective on how each family member has treated him, gaining an understanding of how poor communication and the family's misguided intentions have led Chris to feel like an outsider. By the end of the recording, the family finally realizes how Chris has cried out for their attention, but due to his class clown nature, they cannot be sure if what he does next is another one of his jokes or is in fact real.

Time period: The present.

Chris
15 years old

About the scene: As part of his video to his family, Chris confronts his older brother Brent about their complicated relationship.

Chris:

Now once again, on with the show. No show could be complete without you, Brent. *(Puts a ball cap on backwards.)* The best basketball player to ever play in the state of New York. "Mr. Popularity," "Mr. Can-get-any-girl-he-wants," "Mr.-I-don't-have-to-do-anything-I-don't-want-to-do." Brent, let's talk about you. Everything has always come so easy for you. The looks, the charm, the athletic ability.

Before I came to high school, I was your biggest fan. I was proud to be your brother. I was in awe of you, and my classmates couldn't believe that I got to use the same bathroom as you and even ride the same bus as you.

But when I got to high school, it was pretty obvious you weren't glad to be my brother. You would always go the other direction when you would see me walk anywhere near you. And you'd always say the same thing when anyone asked if we were brothers. *(Covers his head with his hands, mocking Brent, as if he was hearing voices.)* "Unfortunately, yes, but I don't claim him. We're nothing alike." You said it a million times.

You fixed me up with girls you knew would dump me. Popular girls you knew would only make fun of me.

Despite all of that, you're a great guy, and I admire you. I could never compete with you, and to tell you the truth, I never really wanted to. I always wanted a brother, just maybe not the world's greatest everything brother. I just wanted your support and just for once to hear you say, "That's my kid brother."

Mayfair Lady

Adapted by Gary Peterson

About the play: In this fresh adaptation of Shaw's *Pygmalion*, as Cockney-speaking flower girl Eliza Doolittle transforms into a young lady under the tutelage of Professor Higgins and Colonel Pickering, she grows not just intellectually but also emotionally, developing her own personality and pride.

Time period: 1912.

Higgins
40s

About the scene: Colonel Pickering and the housekeeper, Mrs. Pearce, accuse Professor Higgins of trying to bribe Eliza to study under him. They demand he be more honest with her. Here, Higgins lays out in great detail to Eliza what is to be expected of her during the time of her tutelage.

Higgins:

All right, Eliza. You are to live here for the next three months, learning how to speak beautifully and correctly, like a lady in a florist's shop. If you're good and do whatever you're told, you shall sleep in a proper bedroom, and have lots to eat, and money to buy chocolates and take rides in taxis. If you're naughty and idle, you will sleep in the back kitchen among the black beetles and be walloped by Mrs. Pearce with a broomstick.

At the end of three months, you shall go to Buckingham Palace in a carriage, beautifully dressed. If the King finds out you're not a lady, you will be taken by the police to the Tower of London, where you'll be imprisoned as a warning to other presumptuous flower girls. But if you are not found out, you shall have a present of seven-and-sixpence to start a new life as a lady in a shop. If you refuse this offer you will be a most ungrateful and wicked girl, and the angels will weep for you.

(To others.) Now are you satisfied, Pickering? Can I put it more plainly and fairly, Mrs. Pearce?

Doolittle
40s or older

About the scene: Eliza's father has learned of her involvement with Henry Higgins and approaches Higgins and Colonel Pickering expecting a dowry, wrongly assuming Higgins has taken Eliza as a wife. Like Eliza, he speaks with a thick Cockney accent.

Doolittle:

(Unabashed.) Can't afford them, guv'ner. Neither could you if you was as poor as me. Not that I mean any harm, you know. But if Liza is going to have a bit out of this, why not me, too? Look at it this way—what am I, guv'ners, both? I ask you, what am I? I'm one of the undeserving poor, that's what I am! Think of what that means to a man. It means that I'm up agen middle class morality all the time. If there's any monetary assistance to be had, and I puts in for a bit of it, it's always the same story, "You're undeserving, so you can't have it." But my needs is as great as the most deserving widow that ever got money out of six different charities in one week for the death of the same husband. I don't need less than a deserving man, I need more. I don't eat less hearty than him, and I drink—oh, a lot more! Guv'ners, I'm playing straight with you. I ain't pretending to be deserving. I'm undeserving, and I mean to go on being undeserving. I like it. That's the truth. Would you do a man out of the price of his own daughter what he's brought up and

fed and clothed by the sweat of his brow until she's growed big enough to be interesting to you two gentlemen? Is five pounds unreasonable? I put it to you, and I leave it to you.

Memory Garden

By Mark Scharf

About the play: Angie, a young widow with two young daughters, devotes herself to maintaining the roadside memorial for her husband, who died in a tragic hit-and-run car accident. Angie has become such a familiar figure at the site that neighbors beep their horns and wave hello as they pass. When Dan, claiming to be a reporter, stops to get her story, Angie unexpectedly finds the answers to her own questions about what happened on that terrible day.

Time period: The present.

Dan
Late 30s - early 40s

About the scene: After Angie figures out Dan was the driver who killed her husband, he tries to explain what happened on the day of the accident.

Dan:

I didn't know I'd cut him off. I didn't see him. I was just driving home. I just wanted to go home. I got off the exit and looked in the rearview mirror, and there he was ridin' right on my ass.

I couldn't see his eyes behind those sunglasses, but he was shouting at me, and I knew he was really pissed about something. And he looked like he could kill me with his bare hands. He wouldn't back off. I was afraid he was going to follow me all the way home. I was afraid he was going to... I just wanted him to back off. I just wanted him to leave me alone.

I thought if I tapped my brakes he'd back off, but he didn't. I sped up as fast I could, and he just stayed right there. He wouldn't leave me alone, so I... so I slammed on my brakes. And I killed your husband.

I don't expect you to forgive me. You must hate me. I think about it every day. I wake up in the morning and there it is. I try to work and there it is—it's only a thought away every second of every day. I drive by here every day and I remember... And I see you out here and I... I wanted you to know.

The Most Viewed Least Watched Talk Show in History

By Kenneth R. Preuss

About the play: Public-access talk show hosts Brighton and Avery don't have very good guests. Or many regular viewers. Their show, "Monumental Achievements," features anything but, as guest after guest proves to be entirely unexceptional in almost every way. But just as the hosts are about to call it a wrap on another unremarkable show, a special, last-minute guest provides a future perspective that has Brighton and Avery reconsidering everything and wondering if their show might truly wind up being the most viewed someday, even if it is the least watched talk show in history.

Time period: The present.

Quinn
20s

About the scene: One of the talk show guests, Quinn, tells the tale of his monumental achievement with a talking duck.

Quinn:

He's a duck. I named him MacDuck. [...]

It's actually a pun on the name "MacDuff" from the Scottish play. I was reading Shakespeare aloud in the woods when I started to hear my words come back to me. First, I thought it was an echo, but I noticed some ducks across the pond and figured one of them was communicating with me. I decided to call the talking duck over, so I shouted, "Duck!" All the people swimming in the pond went like this. (*Dips quickly, throws hands up defensively, and cowers.*) ...because all the ducks flew over to me, thinking I was calling them. [...]

None of them were talking at first, so I read Shakespeare as I walked along a path, and MacDuck was the only one who followed. Deep in the woods, we set up camp, and we delved into the Bard. We stayed up all night. I recited lines, and MacDuck repeated them. We recited "to be or not to be," "friends, Romans, countrymen," "fair is foul and foul is fair." We really chuckled about that one. You know, since ducks are fowl. It was a transcendent night. But things took a sad turn in the morning. [...]

I got a little... Ambitious. *(Sighs.)* Shakespeare elevates language and explores relevant themes, but everyone knows the greatest form of theatrical expression is... musical theatre. But it didn't go as planned. "Let's start with *Chicago*," I said, and MacDuck moved away a bit. I figured he didn't like Bob Fosse, so I suggested we shift to *Oklahoma*. He moved away even further. MacDuck obviously thought *Chicago* and *Oklahoma* were locations that I was suggesting he migrate to. Thank goodness I didn't say *South Pacific*. *(Builds up dramatically.)* I tried to think of a musical with a non-location title, but made a poor choice in shouting... *Cats!* Anyway, he flew to the top of a tree. I panicked and called out the most innocuous musical I could think of... *Bye Bye Birdie!* *(Softly and sadly.)* And MacDuck, thinking I was bidding farewell, shed a tear... lifted a wing to wave... and flew off, never to be seen again.

◆◆◆

The Nose That Ran Away from Its Face

Adapted by Joseph Robinette

About the play: What happens when a nose cuts loose to spite its face? Inspired by Nikolai Gogol's absurd short story "The Nose," this quirky, comedic journey begins when a giant sneeze separates a young boy and his pun-loving proboscis. The sassy schnozzle celebrates his newfound freedom and the commercial possibilities that come with it, entertaining job offers from an ENT doctor and a florist. Meanwhile, the boy frantically searches for his wandering facial feature and struggles to come to terms with his nose-less identity.

Time period: Timeless.

◆◆◆

Nose
Ageless

About the scene: Following a giant sneeze that opens the play, Nose suddenly appears, having just escaped the face of a boy and finally "running" free on his own.

Nose:

I'm free... I'm free. I'm free! Free at last of those idling eyes, those irritating ears, that muttering mouth, that ugly face. Well, maybe not ugly exactly, but certainly not deserving of such a handsome, classic nose as I.

Notice the noble nostrils, the Romanesque ridge, the symmetrical slope. I am the very model of a perfectly modern proboscis. That means nose. And that's me. And I'm free!

Thank you, oh great maker of sneezes. That was a masterful sneeze that brought my master to his knees and set me free. Now I can go anywhere I please without being tied down anymore. I can wake up in the morning and smell the roses like all the other free noses...

Actually, I've never seen another nose that was free. Maybe I'm the only one. The very first. I could be a world's record. Hello, Mr. Guinness? Stick this nose in your book!

◆◆◆

Boy
Teens

About the scene: Following a giant sneeze that opens the play, Boy discovers he has just lost his Nose. He runs onstage, frantic and with bandaging over where his nose should be.

Boy:

Oh my gosh! Oh my gosh! Has—has anybody seen a nose running around here? A runny nose. Hey, that's kind of funny. A runny nose... No, it's not. It's my nose, and it's run away.

I put too much pepper on my scrambled eggs this morning and sneezed a sneeze like I've never sneezed before. Then I suddenly realized my nose was gone! I looked everywhere in the kitchen—the table, the floor, the countertop, the little shelf where I keep my baseball cards. Everywhere. But the nose was gone.

I took some Silly Putty and put it where the nose used to be, then tied this bandage around it to hold it in place. It looks bad, I know, but it's better than people seeing me without a nose completely. What will I tell them? *(Thinks.)* I know! I cut my nose shaving. But I'm too young to shave. I'll tell them I got in a fight and broke my nose. But that would mean I lost the fight. I'll tell them... I'll tell them something. But I'll have to figure that out later, 'cause right now I've got to follow my nose!

◆◆◆

Paul Bunyan and the Hard Winter

By Wil Denson

About the play: Capturing all the fun of folklore and tall tales, Rip Snortin' Sam tells a young reporter of when Paul Bunyan and his crew of lumberjacks unexpectedly found themselves facing the hardest of hard winters.

Time period: 1891.

Rip Snortin' Sam
Late 20s - early 50s

About the scene: With a mix of bluster and bravado, Rip Snortin' Sam opens the play by introducing himself to the audience and starting to narrate the tall tales about Paul Bunyan.

Rip Snortin' Sam:

(Fiercely.) My name's Rip Snortin' Sam and I kin howl like a wolf and growl like a panther. I kin roar like a bear and snarl like a lion! I'm the strawboss here. The foreman. And they call me Rip Snortin' Sam 'cause I'm a rip snortin' man! Why, I'm the rippin-est, snortin'est man in the whole North Woods! I can out rip and out snort any man alive! *(Suddenly wary, apologetic.)* 'Cept Paul a'course. Paul Bunyan that is. Nobody kin out snort him. Nobody. I worked fer Paul and I know. I worked fer him, oh, about elebendy years ago, and not far from here either. Over by the big lake. You know where I mean!

Now this here's jist a story. So ya don't have ta believe it. Not if ya don't want to. Not all of it anyway. See, some of the stories ya hear about Paul Bunyan are a little "exaggerated." I know that. Like the tall tale about Ol' Paul diggin' out the whole dang Pacific Ocean! Now how could a person believe that? A whole ocean! How could anybody ever believe Paul dug the Pacific? No man could! That ain't possible! Anybody knows it wasn't Paul!

It wuz Paul's big blue ox, Babe, what dug out the Pacific!

And the woods wuz different then, too. Thicker. Lots thicker. The trees stood closer together. Why... why, a man had to walk sideways jist to git between 'em. And a tomcat had to suck in his breath and walk skinny or he'd git his fur caught on the bark! And the seasons of the year wuz different back then, too. We only had two seasons generally... winter and August. And even August wuz coolish. 'Course sometimes it wuz hotter than average, too. Like... like the Summer of the Dry Rain. The Dry Rain that fell up instead of down. Why, it wuz so hot durin' the Summer of the Dry Rain that all the corn standin' out in the fields... popped! The corn popped before you could pick it. And the cows saw all that popcorn and thought it wuz snow. And froze to death right on the spot. Yup, things wuz different back then, all right!

Playground

By Wil Denson

About the play: Playground is an exploration inside the mind of a small child whose life has fallen to pieces at an early age. Jason's dad has recently left him and his mom, and fourth grade is tough; he is constantly bullied by the sixth graders on the playground. Jason attempts to keep to himself, and finds comfort in his imaginary friend Big John, part big brother and part father figure who is very athletic and muscular. Although Big John does his best to cheer him up, he also has the propensity to let Jason down, just like his father.

Time period: 1984.

◆◆◆

Big John
20 years old

About the scene: Big John is constantly trying to cheer up Jason, creating imaginary fantastical situations where he stands up to bullies or dances around with gusto to take Jason away from reality. In this monologue, Big John begins a one-on-one game of basketball, trying to get Jason involved.

Big John:

(With an incredible drawn-out war whoop, Big John scoops up the ball and runs wildly, comically—knees high and pumping head back and bobbing.) Oh, I'm tough! Oh, look out for me! Oh, I'm mean! I'm mean, I'm mean, I'm mean Joe Greene!

(Struts about.) Just look at me and you'll know what meeeeean looks like! Here's meeeeeean. Just put your eyes on what meeeeeeean looks like! *(He freezes, sniffs.)* And smells like.

(Begins to work the ball now, enacting both announcer and expert ball handler, trying to lure Jason into the game. He dribbles

expertly, faking, circling Globetrotter fashion, all the while doing running commentary.)

And we're all tied at ninety-six with less than a minute to go. Boston needs this one, folks. Magic Johnson brings the ball down slowly. Twenty-five seconds left in the ball game. He moved to his right looking for an opening. Look at that big guy handle the ball! Milwaukee's afraid to even come out on him! He keeps moving, keeps moving. But they just won't come out. Come on, Milwaukee! *(Trying to get Jason into one-on-one.)*

Milwaukee must know the Magic Man can hit from out, but they hold back. We don't know why. He fakes left, fakes right. Look at Johnson, he's a one-man show out there! He's letting the clock run down, waiting for one last shot! Ten seconds! Nine! The crowd is going wild! Five seconds! And there he goes! Magic Johnson's going in! *(Does a wonderful series of turns, changes of dribbling hands, and fakes, and takes the ball in for the winning layup. Then, arms high, he prances the full stage in a victory celebration.)*

He scores! Magic Johnson scores! The game's over and Boston wins it! Ninety-eight, ninety-six. What a game, folks! And what a guy that Magic Johnson is! It's clear who won this game! Magic... Magic... Magic! *(Stops, drops his arms, blows hard a few times to get his breath and crosses to Jason. He puts the ball on the ground and sits on it.)* Whew! Tough game. Too bad, Milwaukee. Good try but you should have come out on me.

◆◆◆

Poe: Dreams of Madness

By Allyssa Hynes

About the play: It's nearly midnight and our troubled protagonist, famed author Edgar Allan Poe, is having difficulty sleeping... or at least he thinks he is. With the Raven acting as a grim and mischievous tour guide, both the positively dead and the presumed living give breath to thrilling Poe retellings, including "The Tell-Tale Heart," "The Fall of the House of Usher," "The Pit and the Pendulum," "The Masque of the Red Death," "The Raven," and more.

Time period: 1840s.

◆◆◆

Edgar Allan Poe
30s

About the scene: Opening up the play, Poe sets the scene of this tale of madness, drifting between the blur of wakefulness and sleep.

Poe:

I am haunted by dreams, even when I wake. And so I wander in this dazed stupor, unsure if I am awake or asleep, unsure if I am alive. No... I must be alive, for I am alone. Always alone. *(Feels a draft and closes the open window.)* I thought I had found surcease of sorrow with my wife. But instead, torment. She is dying, and I will lose her. Or have I lost her already? *(Sits again at his desk.)*

I fear I have lost my sanity. I am not myself. Where am I now? Richmond, where I grew up with the Allans? Boston, where I was born? Philadelphia? Baltimore, where I will...? Or am I stuck in a nightmare? That seems most likely. What time does it say? *(Looks at grandfather clock.)* Near midnight. That seems like a fitting setting for one of my stories. Perhaps a story from which I cannot escape. Midnight. *(Ponders the idea.)* Once upon a midnight... *(Searches for the right word.)* Creepy? No. A midnight... sorrowful? No. Once upon a midnight squishy? Not at all! Dark? Bleak? Eerie? No, not quite it. A midnight... *(Thinks, then sees Raven.)* A midnight of madness! *(Watches as Raven moves forward and slowly starts to dance. He is enraptured by Raven's dance and receives inspiration. He shuffles his papers, ready to write.)* Once upon a midnight... *(Becomes frazzled when he can't find something to write with.)* No quills. There's nothing to write with, even if there were something to write! *(Slams the papers down on the desk, and Raven abruptly stops dancing.)* What vision is this? What is your purpose? What do you want? *(Twirls in his seat and stares at Raven, unnerved.)* Ebony bird, leave my loneliness unbroken. Let me be! *(Raven does not move. Poe cowers.)*

Abandoned by those I love to be haunted by a demon bird. These visions would not appear if I were not alone. Why do those I need depart from me? My wife, Virginia. My savior. She and my mother-in-law, Muddy, providing the family I always sought. Some moments of pure happiness. Until one night, mid-song... I learned she would not be long for this world. Much as I tried to deny it, she would be like the others.

My own mother, Eliza Poe, an actress, gave a moving death scene before me when I was a child. And Fanny Allan, the woman who would raise me, succumbed to illness as well.

For, alas—alas!—with me
The light of life is o'er!
No more, no more, no more—
Such language holds the solemn sea
To the sands upon the shore,

Shall bloom the thunder-blasted tree,
Or the stricken eagle soar!

And all my days are trances,
And all my nightly dreams
Are where thy grey eye glances,
And where thy footstep gleams—
In what ethereal dances,
By what eternal streams.

I can feel their presence. It is but fear that keeps them from me.
I am going mad, I fear. Like the characters in my stories.

Pollyanna

Adapted by Susan Pargman

About the play: This is the classic tale of the greatest optimist of all time... Pollyanna. Pollyanna becomes an orphan, and she is placed into the care of her purely pessimistic and domineering aunt. The town itself isn't much better. Led by a fire and brimstone pastor whose favorite Bible verse is "Woe unto you," folks are always complaining, feeling sorry for themselves, and viewing their existence as dark and dreary. Yet, Pollyanna faithfully plays her "Glad Game," innocently teaching it to others wherever she goes.

Time period: 1910.

Jimmy Bean
10 years old

About the scene: Jimmy Bean has just run away from the orphanage where he has lived most of his life. He is currently on the hunt for a family and a new place to live. As Pollyanna is walking home, she runs into Jimmy Bean and, after introducing herself, she asks where he lives, to which he replies "Nowhere." Curious about this response, she peppers him with more questions and challenges him to talk more.

Jimmy Bean:

All right, then, here goes! I'm Jimmy Bean and I'm ten years old goin' on eleven. I come last year to live at the Orphans' Home. But they've got so many kids, there ain't much room for me, an' I wasn't never wanted, anyhow, I don't believe. So I've quit. I'm goin' to live somewheres else. But I hain't found the place, yet. I'd like a home—just a common one, y'know—with a mother in it, instead of a Matron. If ya has a home, ya has folks; an' I hain't had folks since Dad died. So I'm a-huntin' now. I've tried four houses, but they didn't want me, though I said I expected to work, 'course. There! Is that all you want to know, Miss Busybody?

Pride and Prejudice
Adapted by Rebecca Gellott

About the play: This superbly written adaptation restores many popular scenes and conversations from the book that are often cut from other screen and stage adaptations. Revisit all your favorite characters here: witty, free-spirited Elizabeth Bennet and her four sisters, including the lovely Jane; Mrs. Bennet, who only wants what's best for her daughters; Mr. Bennet, who has made it his life's work to affectionately make sport of his wife; and of course, the suitors, Mr. Darcy, Charles Bingley, and George Wickham.

Time period: Early 1800s.

Mr. Darcy
20s - 30s

About the scene: Mr. Darcy finally musters up the courage to ask Elizabeth to marry him, much to her surprise. He is smitten with Elizabeth, finding her to be of equal wit and virtue as him and only wishes to have the honor of her hand in marriage. Caught up in sharing his own feelings, he is completely unaware of the condescending tone of his proposal.

Mr. Darcy:

Miss Bennet. I… That is, might I inquire… *(Lays his hat down on settee and takes a deep breath. Then, almost businesslike, with words rushing forth.)* In vain, I have struggled. It will not do. You must allow me to tell you how ardently I admire and love you. *(Elizabeth's jaw drops. He continues, fervently.)*

From almost our first meeting in Hertfordshire, I have failed to repress my feelings. They are born of such passion that I could hardly find the words to speak in front of you for fear of giving myself away or giving you false hope of receiving my attentions. Your liveliness of mind, Miss Bennet. The severity of your wit. Your eyes... have me utterly defeated.

(Continues as if reassuring her.) I am conscious of your inferiority of station, the degradation I am sure to endure in the eyes of society, and the objectionable nature of your whole family whose condition in life is so decidedly beneath my own. Nevertheless, I have formed so affectionate an attachment as to be unable to conquer it despite my better judgment. I hope now to be relieved of my anxiety and rewarded by your accepting my hand in marriage. *(Ends up beside her, holding his hand out expectantly with a sigh of relief.)*

Quaran-Teens

By Laurie Allen

About the play: This play consists of 15 four- to seven-minute original monologues that explore a variety of teen responses to the pandemic and the safer-at-home restrictions that came with it. From restoring old friendships and keeping traditions alive to missing baseball, graduation, prom, and so much more, each character portrays an arc to move past their anger, disappointment, and bitterness and show the resiliency of teens. Each monologue offers a unique, true-to-life point of view of this real-world crisis that maintains an element of hope for a brighter future.

Time period: 2020.

Josh
16 – 18

About the scene: The high school student, cooped up at home because of the pandemic, reflects on his relationship with his elderly neighbor as he sits on his front porch, eating a cookie.

Josh:

Mrs. Evans can't figure me out. She's this super old lady who lives across the street from me. And when I say old, I mean old! And did I mention unfriendly? Yeah, that too. But now... *(Takes another bite.)* She doesn't know what to think about me. I know what she used to think about me. "Disrespectful teen."

Why? I'll tell you why. Because I drilled holes in the muffler of my car. *(Smiles proudly.)* Oh, yeah. It's loud and powerful. So, picture this. Loud music, loud muffler... yeah, bringing it home. Sometimes, before leaving the house, I rev it up. Oh, yeah, I let it go! Mrs. Evans, well, she slams her door shut, but not before glaring at me and shaking her head. "Hey, old

woman, wanna see me do a donut right in front of your house?"
Yeah, I'd like to show her who's all that! Call me the bad teen in
the neighborhood if you want to. I don't care. But I've gotta be
careful. Because my dad, if he catches me driving too fast, he'd
pull the keys from me. But I can still make some noise, can't I?
Oh, yeah!

Well, that was before. Before I was stuck at home. Where can
I go now? Nowhere. It's like the whole world is grounded. So
here I sit, on my front porch, wondering how long this will last.
When will the stupid virus just die so I can get back to tearing
up the streets? "Hey, Mrs. Evans, I feel your pain! I'm stuck
at the house just like you! I'm not going anywhere, either. Just
like you! So, maybe I'll shut my door, too! Shut out the world!
Just like you."

But last week, Mrs. Evans messed up. Her little white barking
poodle—who, trust me, is more annoying than my booming
muffler—ran out the door. Mrs. Evans was checking her mail
and her dog, Peanut, ran for it! I guess Peanut was sick of being
quarantined, too. I get it. The dog sees an opening and goes for
it. Free-dom! Darts out the door and runs down the street like
there's a marathon to be won. Good thing I'm not out driving
that day. That could've been the end of Peanut.

So, I see Mrs. Evans standing at her front door looking
distraught. "Peanut, Peanut! Get back here!" she says. Mrs.
Evans has a walker, so it's not like she can go running after it.
And here I am, standing in the yard eating an ice cream cone
because Mom doesn't like them dripping in the house. So, what
do I do? I drop the cone in the grass and take off. "Fluffy, get
back here!" I scream. Dumb dog! She's zigging and zagging…
running from one side of the street to the other. A couple cars

even have to slam on their brakes to miss her. Again, it's a good thing I wasn't driving that day!

So, you have to understand, I play football. I'm in it to win it! I'm going to tackle that dog! *(Falls forward.)* "Gotcha!" *(Sits back up.)* Yes! I got her! Peanut is panting, and I am, too. "Gotcha, girl!" We both take a minute to catch our breath, then she starts licking me to death. "You're safe now, girl. Let's go home." So, I walk three blocks back to the house carrying this football... trophy... or whatever you wanna call it... dog... back to Mrs. Evans. I knock on her door, then step back... you know the six feet thing... and then she opens the door. Well, you should've seen her face! Not the usual irritated, angry look, but tears are flowing down her face. I think they were sad tears that turned into happy tears. Mrs. Evans pulls a tissue from the pocket of her robe and quickly wiped them away. I didn't know what to say.

Then, with her walker in tow, she starts inching her way towards me. "No, stay there." I tell her. Quickly, I open her front door and give the runaway dog a gentle push back inside her house. "There you go," I say. Then, this old woman looks deep into my eyes and says... "Thank you. She's my only... she's my best friend."

Then, all of a sudden, I gotta blink fast to keep stupid tears falling down my face! I don't wanna look like a sissy!

◆◆◆

Rememberin' Stuff

By Eleanor Harder

About the play: When a group of high school drama students is given the assignment to share their memories with each other, the result is an eclectic collection of hilarious, heartfelt, serious, intense, and inspiring scenes and monologues.

Time period: The present.

Billy
Teens

About the scene: Billy remembers a time his mom had to use food stamps at the grocery store. As he retells this unpleasant memory, we hear his pain turn to determination as he recalls how others openly judged their family. (NOTE: As a monologue, the actor also delivers the lines of his mother.)

Billy:

When I think of food, I think of food stamps. I remember when my dad was sick and my mom had been laid off her job and things were really bad at home. Well, one day I went to the market with my mom. And as we were standing in line to pay for our groceries, Mom was having trouble getting the food stamps out of her wallet, and she dropped one. She was nervous, I guess. I mean, she wasn't used to those stamps. Anyhow, there were these two older people behind us in line—a man and his wife, I guess. And I remember when they saw the food stamps, they started shakin' their heads and givin' out these big sighs 'cuz it was taking Mom so long. And they were lookin' over our groceries, which were just sitting there being checked through, and they were talking to each other, sort of soft, but loud enough for us to hear, which was the idea. [...]

"Them." *(Slight grin, shakes head.)* I wasn't very old, but I knew that meant us—us, and all the poor people like us. I know Mom heard, too, but she just stood up straight and tall and paid the cashier with the stamps, and then said—

"Come on, Billy."

We picked up our groceries and went out to the car. I saw that Mom looked like she was about to cry. Only she didn't. We got in and closed the car doors. And then she said—

"I want you to know something, Billy. It wasn't always like this with us, and it isn't always gonna be, neither. Just remember that, hear?"

Then she gunned the motor of that old pick-up we had, *(Makes gunning noises.)* and we took off for home faster'n we'd ever done before! Like Mom said, I did remember what she told me. I always will, because you just don't forget something like that.

David
Teens

About the scene: David tells his friends about his months-long quest to get Debbie to notice him. From dropping his book at her feet—or rather, on her foot—to reading Shakespeare in English class, David thought he had tried it all. That is, until a new opportunity presented itself.

David:

Talkin' about kids and all reminds me of something. Couple of weeks ago I was walking downtown and I saw this bookstore window that had all these kids' books in it. Y'know, like *Peter Rabbit* and *Winnie the Pooh* and *Wizard of Oz*. All that stuff. Well, I'm standing there, remembering how I really liked those books when I was a little kid. And I'm grinning and staring in at these things. And suddenly I look up and I see Debbie Fineman, who's inside the store, and she's looking out the window and grinning and staring at me! Well, like, I'm dyin' of embarrassment. See, I've been trying to get Debbie Fineman's attention ever since she showed up in my English class two months ago. I mean, I did everything. I raised my hand every time Mr. Armstrong asked a question, even if I didn't know the answer, which was usually the case.

And then I gave a really Oscar-winning reading of Romeo in class. Anyway, I thought it was. *(Recites with volume and great emotion.)* "But soft, what light through yonder window breaks? It is the east, and Juliet is the sun!" *(Shrugs.)* Total nothing. Then I tried dropping my Shakespeare book at her feet, like it was an accident.

I didn't mean for it to fall right on her foot. But it did. And still nothing. Like, our eyes never even met. 'Course, I was leaning down, trying to pick up my book and muttering how sorry I was.

Meantime, she's walking away. Well, limping away. By then, I'd have settled for her just knowing I existed on this planet! Which, despite everything, I do not think she was aware of. Okay, so now I'm lookin' in at the kiddie section of the bookstore, which is not the way I want to get Debbie Fineman's attention. Right?

Well, I mean, I'm tryin' to look suave, despite my face, which is now burning up. So I go into my best Humphrey Bogart stance that I remember from those old movies, and I say, *(Imitates Bogart.)* "Not really, sweetha't, I was just passin' by on my way to meet Sidney Greenstreet."

And then, I don't know, we just got to jabberin' away about kids' books, and remembering all the stories and the pictures and stuff. And before you know it, we're sittin' in Pizza Hut, havin' pizza and Coke and talking about *Babar the Elephant*, for crying out loud! For months I only fantasized about having a date with Debbie Fineman. I was too chicken to even think about asking her out. And then, here we get together on account of Eeyore and Piglet and the Tin Man and Toto! *(Shrugs.)* Go figure, huh?

Pete
Teens

About the scene: Pete remembers the first play he was ever in, which happened to be a disaster.

Pete:

Hey, wait! When you said drama class, that reminded me of the first play I was ever in.

I remember I was playing a king, and I wore this long, heavy robe with fake fur all around and a big gold crown painted like it had jewels all over it. Really cool. Anyhow, Mrs. Johnson told me not to slouch because kings stand up straight and hold their heads up high. Makes them look regal, she says. Then she tells me to speak my lines—all three of them —with authority, and to practice being regal.

Right. So, I went home and I practiced looking regal in front of the bathroom mirror. But, y'know, if you hold your head clear up *(Demonstrates.)*, it's kind of hard to see yourself in the mirror. But I felt I looked pretty regal. And in the bathroom my opening line, "Pages, prepare the feast!" sounded fantastic!

I mean, like Lawrence Olivier! Sort of. *(Sighs.)* So, anyhow, comes the night of the big performance, and the parents and, you know, all kinds of people are in the audience. *(Peers out as if from behind curtains.)* Oh, no. Look at all of them out there, just waiting for me to fail!

Well, by now I'm feeling sick to my stomach I'm so nervous and wondering why I ever tried out for this stupid play in the first place. Then Mrs. Johnson yells, "Places, everybody!"

So, Wanda Turner, who's playing the queen, is standing next to me, and the trumpeters and the pages are all in place onstage, and the curtains open and it's time for my big entrance. Trumpets blaring, the whole bit. And I start in, remembering what Mrs. Johnson said about being regal, and boy, am I being regal! *(Demonstrates.)* I mean, I've got my head up so high I didn't see the little footstool on the stage in front of me. Suddenly, I tripped over the thing, getting myself all tangled up in my robe in the process. So I'm staggering around the stage, and I knock one trumpeter off his feet. He bumps into the other one, who crashes through the flimsy throne we have. I make a grab for the stage curtain, which rips apart and comes crashing down with me in a humongous cloud of dust!

Well, I mean, there's this great big gasp from the audience, and Mrs. Johnson looks like she's going to faint, and Wanda Turner bursts into tears, and I'm sitting there in a cloud of dust with the stage curtain all over me wondering what desert island I can instantly escape to. And then, I don't know, out of somewhere I get this brainstorm. And I crawl out from under the curtain and I turn to my pages, who are standing there totally frozen, and I say, regally and with authority, "Pages, clear up this mess!" Well, like, the whole audience begins laughing and whistling and applauding. And Mrs. Johnson is grinning, and Wanda Turner stops bawling, and I'm sitting there, hearing this magical sound coming up to me over the footlights and it's—it's like nothing I ever heard before. And right then I'm hooked. Totally. *(Stands, brushes himself off.)*

Now you might not think that that particular moment would be a good time to make a lifetime career choice. And you'd be right. But I remember it's how and when I decided to become an actor.

◆◆◆

Tony
18 years old

About the scene: A teenage alcoholic downplays his addiction while recalling the nearly tragic event that brought him into rehab. Passing through layers of denial and making light of his problem, Tony eventually discloses a fundamental fault in his character that casts doubt on his chances of recovery.

Tony:

Yeah, I share an interest. Share it with a lot of people. Alcohol. So, okay, what's that got to do with the price of beans? Well, 'cause I'm rememberin' stuff—rememberin' when I got busted for drunk driving. Everybody says I was lucky not to get myself killed or kill somebody else. And I know I was lucky 'cause the car was totaled. So, for a while I got smart and quit driving when I was drinkin'. *(Grins.)* But I was still drinkin'. Y'know, man, I mean—it helps you forget your problems. Well, *(Shrugs.)* helped me, anyhow.

So, like, I don't remember when I started. I just know I'd drink anything in sight that had alcohol in it, anytime I could find it. Which wasn't hard. Not at my old man's place. Hell, it was easier to find his booze than to find him. So anyhow, now I'm in one of those counseling programs. You know, for *(Makes quotation marks in the air with his fingers.)* "substance abusers." I didn't think alcohol counted as a "substance." I mean, we got potheads and speed freaks and you name it in our program. But my counselors, I don't know, they consider alcohol a substance, and me a substance abuser. Well, actually, my official title is "an alcoholic." Hey, at my age I got a title already. It's an okay program. I mean, if it can keep me from windin' up like my old man, who's a real loser, then I'm willin' to give it a try. For a while, anyhow. You know, see how it goes. I haven't had a drink this time around for three months. Three months and sixteen days, to be exact. So, no big deal, you say, huh? Well, for an "alcoholic substance abuser" it is a big deal, lemme tell ya. *(Nods, as if to himself.)*

So, okay, why did I get started drinking in the first place? I don't remember that. I mean, some things you remember, and some things you don't. Right? I've thought about it, but—well, there's this little story I really like. Says a lot, I think. See, there's these two twins, and some dude says to one of 'em, "Hey, Joe, how come you drink?" And Joe says, "'Cause my old man's an alcoholic." And then this dude asks the other twin, "Hey, Moe, how come you don't drink?" And Moe says, "'Cause my old man's an alcoholic." *(Chuckles.)* Yeah. I like that one. *(Shrugs.)* So, guess I'm the first twin, huh?

◆◆◆

The Reunion

By Doug Jockinsen

About the play: This is a rich story of a young couple, a handyman and a cleaning woman from Saudi Arabia, and a small tapestry that ties all their lives together even if they don't know it. Fate, a bit of luck, and the belief that those who do for others deserve that gift in return conspire to join forces and lead to an ending that is sure to warm their hearts.

Time period: 2021.

Ali
Late 50s

About the scene: After noticing his wife's tapestry hanging in the young couple's apartment, Saudi handyman Ali explains to the tapestry's current owner, Jill, why he recognized it immediately and why he does not want it back.

Ali:

My wife and I are— were both Saudis by birth and educated in British schools. We were visiting colleagues in Baghdad when the Gulf War bombing began thirty years ago. We tried to drive to the Kuwaiti border to escape, but the traffic was backed up for a mile and our car ran out of gas before we got there. We pulled off the road, took what we could of our belongings from the car, put them into a basket, and... *(Points to the tapestry.)* ...used that very tapestry to cover the basket.

In the chaos and the bombing, we became separated trying to run to the Kuwaiti border. I waited for her there for as long as I could, until the American troops said that it was too dangerous and that I had to leave. Several hundred of us were airlifted out. We had to leave all we had brought with us there at the border.

That was the last day I ever saw her. I waited at the refugee camp for her to arrive. Every day I looked for her to come, but she never did. I assume she was caught and killed by the Republican Guard.

That, as they say, was a long, long time ago, and thousands of miles away. There is nothing to be said. [...]

It was once a gift given with love and now it is again. My wife would have thought that was a beautiful and proper thing. And she would never want a gift given in love to be taken back. The memory of my wife will forever be here. *(Holds his hand over his heart.)* Let it be a symbol of love in a house where love lives.

The Scarlet Letter
Adapted by Gary W. Abbott

About the play: This play is a faithful adaptation of Nathaniel Hawthorne's powerful drama that takes place in Puritan Boston. Adulteress Hester Prynne must wear a scarlet "A" to mark her shame and secrecy, as she refuses to identify the father of her daughter, Pearl. When Roger Chillingworth, her husband who all thought was lost at sea, arrives in Boston, he reveals his identity to no one but Hester as he seeks revenge on whoever compromised her reputation. Meanwhile, the young, eloquent minister Arthur Dimmesdale is suffering from severely declining health, apparently brought on by great psychological distress. Chillingworth becomes Dimmesdale's physician and eventually moves in with him in order to provide round-the-clock medical attention.

Time period: 1700s.

Arthur Dimmesdale
Mid 30s or older

About the scene: Arthur Dimmesdale has just emerged from giving a powerful sermon in church. Townspeople are all moving toward the town hall for a meal, but Dimmesdale instead seeks out Hester and Pearl, standing near the scaffold. Seeing that he is near death, Hester reminds him that they once planned to die together, but Dimmesdale conveys his wish that she and Pearl both live while he confesses his sin to the town.

Arthur Dimmesdale:

(To Hester.) Nay, for both you and little Pearl, let it be as God shall order—and God is merciful. Hester, I am a dying man. Let me make haste now to take my shame upon me.

(To the crowd.) People of New England! You that have loved me! You that have deemed me holy! Behold me here!

(The crowd is stilled.) At last, I stand upon the spot where years since I should have stood. Here with this woman, whose strength sustains me, at this dreadful moment. Look you all, the scarlet letter which Hester wears! It has long cast a gleam of horrible awe round about her and you have shuddered at it. But there stood one in the midst of you, at whose mark of sin you have not shuddered, though it was on him!

(Directly to Chillingworth.) The Devil knew it well and fretted it continually with the touch of his burning finger. But the wearer hid it cunningly from you and walked among you with the aspect of one mournful because so pure in a sinful world! Now, at the hour of his death, he stands up before you! He bids you look again at Hester's scarlet letter! He tells you that it is but the shadow of what he bears on his own breast, and that even this, his own red stigma, is no more than the type of what has seared his inmost heart! Behold the dreadful witness of it! *(He tears open his shirt.)*

◆◆◆

Scheherazade

Adapted by Susan Pargman

About the play: In the ancient Arabian world, Scheherazade is called upon to use her tale-spinning talents to save her people from certain destruction. Betrayed by his betrothed, the hot-tempered King Raynah decides to punish all the women in his kingdom. Each day he will marry one of them, only to have her beheaded the next morning. Scheherazade is determined to change the fate of these wives with her stories. Armed only with her wit and a smattering of magic, Scheherazade recites her stories for the king himself. Her enchanted tale transforms the king into his own worst enemy: a woman. By the final curtain, the king has become a victim of his own revengeful plot!

Time period: 700 BC.

◆◆◆

Grand Vizier
40s or older

About the scene: The Grand Vizier is both the father to Scheherazade and the main advisor to King Raynah. Here, the concerned parent tells a parable to his daughter. The message of his story is clear: it is a fool's errand to wed the king in hopes of changing him.

Grand Vizier:

I begin my tale with the greatest of pleasure. *(He bows.)* It is said, most wise and faithful Daughter, that once there was a prosperous and wealthy farmer who lived in the countryside and labored on his farm. This man owned a fine ox, who was a strong and willing worker, and a donkey. The wealthy farmer happened to know the secret of understanding the language of beasts. He overheard a conversation one day between these two humble barnyard animals.

(As the ox.) "Oh, Watchful One..." said the ox to the donkey. "I hope that you are enjoying the service you are getting. Your ground is swept, they feed you sifted barley, and offer you cool, fresh water to drink."

(As the donkey.) "Yes, it is true," answered the fortunate donkey.

(As the ox.) "On the contrary, I am taken out to plow the fields day and night, whipped and offered beans soiled with mud. Why am I not treated with kindness, as you are?"

(As donkey.) "It is because you exert and exhaust yourself to comfort others. Why don't you take a lesson from me? When they take you out in the field, kick with your hooves and butt with your head. Then when they offer you beans to eat, don't eat them. Just sniff at them and then turn away. If you do this, life will be better and kinder to you, and you will find relief."

All this conversation took place, Daughter, while the farmer listened and understood. On the following day he took the ox, placed the yoke upon his head and worked him at the plow. The ox followed the donkey's advice and kicked his hooves and butted with his head. When the farmer offered him beans, the ox only sniffed at them and turned away. So the farmer returned the ox to the stable. Instead of the ox, he placed the yoke on the head of the donkey. And forced him to work all day, plowing the fields until they were done.

That night, the donkey returned to the stable, tired and worn from plowing all day. While the ox, who had been resting and chewing cud, invoked many blessings upon the donkey when he returned.

And you, my Daughter, will likewise perish because of your miscalculation. Don't expose yourself to peril. I advise you out of compassion for you.

Shakespeare by Monkeys
By Kamron Klitgaard

About the play: Some theories are nearly impossible to test, such as the Infinite Monkey Theorem, which states that a monkey, randomly hitting keys on a typewriter for an infinite amount of time, will eventually produce the complete works of William Shakespeare. Well, infinity isn't standing in the way of Dr. Hubble, who's determined to prove the theory correct by assembling a cast of zany assistants and six monkeys, whose only job is to get writing using a variety of writing devices!

Time period: The present.

Riley
20s - 30s

About the scene: Lab assistant Riley explains what motivated him to sign up for the project.

Riley:

No! I don't care about the money. I have a more noble purpose—I hate William Shakespeare!

In high school, they made us memorize Shakespeare passages and then recite them in front of the class. I'll never forget it... "This trusty servant shall pass between us. Ere long you are like to hear—if you dare venture in your own behalf—a mistress's command. Wear this. Spare speech. Decline your head. This kiss, if it durst speak, would stretch thy spirits up into the air."

And when I asked my teacher what it meant, she read the passage over several times, and then finally looked up at me and said, "I don't know." I don't know! Can you believe that? She's making me memorize it, and she doesn't even know what it means! It turns out that none of my college professors knew what it meant, either! I searched for the answer online. I searched for it in books. I took Shakespeare classes. No one in the world knows what it means!

But he's considered to be one of the greatest writers ever to live. He's forced on us in elementary school, middle school, high school, college! His plays are performed year after year the world over. Yet, he writes this incomprehensible dribble!

I figured if a monkey could write the complete works of William Shakespeare, then anybody could, proving he's no big deal.

Sir Huey and the Dragon

By Ryan Neely

About the play: Widowed King Arbitrary wants to find a husband for Princess Arabella and decides to do so in the most clueless way possible—pitting two knights against each other in feats of unimaginable danger and unlikely strength. But the wishy-washy king favors flashy Sir Truly over humble Sir Huey and stacks the deck against the nobler knight, sending him on a wild goose chase. Sir Huey still stands a fighting chance thanks to some help from a mysterious helmeted hero and some primitive tree gnomes. But it's Princess Arabella, who's in love with Sir Huey, who helps him in his quest for the heart of the fiery dragon.

Time period: Once upon a time…

Dragon
Ageless

About the scene: After eating the evil Sir Truly, Dragon calls on the village to change their ways and for King Arbitrary to allow his daughter to marry the righteous Sir Huey.

Dragon:

(Commandingly.) Everyone stop!

I'd like to say something. I believe… I believe you should all take a close look at yourselves and what you are doing. Is this really solving anything?

(Burps loudly.) Listen, if you'll just overlook the fact that I ate that cheating, lying knight, there is something to be said about non-violent resolutions. You, King Arbitrary, began all of this so that you could find someone worthy of your daughter's hand. Your daughter is already far braver than any of your knights because she fights for change. Well, I say, if being worthy of her

hand means to stand by her side, who is more worthy than the one man who shares her ideals? Who fights for truth and honor? Who cares not to kill wrongly? You can see that they have already chosen to stand by one another. Perhaps if you grant them the freedom to stay together, then together they can slay the true monster of this kingdom's narrow-minded intolerance and lack of unity. For you can't have strength in numbers if you don't allow those numbers to add up to anything. That's all...

(Burps.) Does anyone have an antacid?

Struggling for the Surface

By Emilio Iasiello

About the play: "Seven years and every year it gets harder," Mary tells her husband, Joe, as they stare down at the grave of their daughter, Maddie, on what would have been her seventeenth birthday. A stranger stops by, seemingly there to pay respects of his own. But before long, Joe comes to find that James is no random visitor. Instead, he's the brother of the drunk driver who killed Joe's precious daughter.

Time period: The present.

Joe
40s

About the scene: Mary has just walked away from her daughter's grave to take some time for herself, leaving Joe to talk with the stranger who has recently come by. Joe shares some sweet memories as well as the tragic details of how his daughter was killed.

Joe:

(About his wife.) Sweetest woman ever put on this green earth. It's hard for her on these days. Sometimes I wonder if it isn't better to just forget. *(Turns to James.)* Of course, it isn't really. But sometimes I wonder.

Sometimes… She's usually not this bad. But today, well, today is her—our daughter's—birthday. *(Gestures to the grave.)*

Seventeen. Each year we mark her birthday with something different. Earrings for her thirteenth birthday. A toy car for when she would have gotten her driver's license. *(Removes a corsage from his pocket and lays it on the grave.)* A corsage for her prom. It's silly I know, but it makes us feel like we're still parents.

Anyway, that's the way it is.

Do you have any childre— I'm sorry, that's prying. [...]

The joy a child brings... well, it's indescribable. With Maddie, there wasn't a day that the sun didn't rise and set on her. And it's funny what you remember. The little things, I mean. Seemingly insignificant at the time, they're the memories that come out of nowhere and make you smile in the middle of the day. Or night. *(Chuckles.)* Like this one time, when she was eight? She made Mary and me breakfast in bed. Thing was, she didn't separate the egg from the shell! They were the darned crunchiest eggs we ever ate in our lives, but we ate them just the same. *(Sighs as the memory fades, along with his smile.)* There isn't a day that goes by when I wouldn't give my right arm for some of those crunchy eggs... *(Stares off.)* [...]

She was playing across the street with her friend, Missy Walters. The two of them were playing dolls. And I remember hearing the car. I was in the living room watching the ball game, and I remember hearing the skid of car tires. I jumped right up, but I was already too late. It was all my worst fears realized. The driver had skidded off the road and took out both girls. One moment they were there, playing, the next, all that's left were these two broken dolls. *(Chokes up.)* He... he... killed them! He killed them both. *(Tears threaten, but Joe fights them off in a way that shows he's had practice.)* I try not to cry for her anymore. She's in a better place. I have to be strong for Mary. Only one of us can afford to grieve. The living must live—I believe that, I really do. Even if it is your flesh and blood that passes. The living owe it to them.

◆◆◆

James
30s

About the scene: James and Joe stand in a cemetery looking over the grave of Joe's deceased daughter who was killed by a drunk driver. In this monologue, James tells Joe about his brother, a rough and irresponsible bad seed who constantly found himself in trouble. In the process, James reveals that it was his brother who killed Joe's daughter and that he blames himself for triggering the sequence of events that ended with the fatal car accident.

James:

I had a brother once. He was, uh, sort of a bad seed. The family embarrassment—you probably know the type. Trouble followed him around like toilet paper on the bottom of his shoe.

It didn't always used to be like that. There were a few years there when he was a pretty decent kid. I mean, children aren't born bad, right? Babies don't come into this world to cause suffering. I just don't believe that. Things happen to make them that way.

I mean, if you want to get right down to it, he picked up a lot of bad traits from our father. That man was a trouble-maker in his day, start to finish. And the apple doesn't fall far from the tree—isn't that what they say? So when the old man died, well, my brother seemed to pick up where he left off.

There were certain… complications. Incidents, you might say. Things that meant little on their own, but when taken together, painted an ugly picture of my brother. There was theft around the house, calls at all hours of the night. And the lies—so many lies that the truth was suffocated! But, blood is blood, right? Even if it's bad.

You love someone, you try to help them. You love them for the good and the bad... But love can be an exhausting thing. I mean, what if... what if the bad stuff starts to outweigh the good? What are you supposed to do then? Do you just give up on them, pretend that they never existed? Do you tell them to walk away and that you never want to see them again?

Well, that's what I did. And everyone supported my decision. It was the right decision. Tough love, that's what my brother needed. He needed to straighten out his act. So early one morning, I called him up. I told him to come right over, that we had things to discuss.

(As he remembers.) It was early, and already he had been drinking. So, I didn't even let him into the house. He'd used up his last chance, I told him. Push had finally met shove. The stealing, the lying—everything—I couldn't take it anymore. And so I told him that morning, I never wanted to see him again, that I didn't want him around my family. I didn't want him. We were no longer brothers, I said.

Oh, he tried to make amends, but I had heard it all before. That's the thing with lies. They go round and round like a skipping record. His promises just didn't hold water anymore, and I told him as much. And then he just got all quiet. And I could see he was breaking up inside, that pieces of him were just crumbling. And then he turned away from me and got into his red Mustang and drove away. *(Joe reacts when he hears it was a red Mustang.)*

My wife and kids stood at the window. They looked so sad and still, just like a painting. And this cold, hard pit had formed in my stomach. It just sat there. And I knew right then I'd made the biggest mistake of my life. [...]

All I've got to go by is what the police report said, but that's when he made the biggest mistake of his life. He tried to hold up a gas station and instead killed two clerks. And then he went on to... [...]

So, you see, I don't know how someone can blame a person for anything. For the past seven years, I've known I should take the blame for the deaths that day. I've had a long time to think about it, and it's the only thing that makes sense. *(Pause.)* Want to know what love is? Love is unconditional. Love isn't just trying to make people better than they are, it's about making yourself better than who you are. And helping the rest.

Stuck

By Jon Jory

About the play: This play takes place in the COVID era, during a stay-at-home order. Each character is school-aged and shares their feelings of being stuck at home. Some are bored and eager for any human interaction outside their family, while others are quite productive in what they're doing with their time while cooped up at home.

Time period: 2020.

Unnamed
Teens

About the scene: The speaker remembers the loss of his sister.

Unnamed:

About two weeks after they said people had to stay home, we found out my sister wasn't going to make it. She had something they call Reye's syndrome that causes swelling in the liver and brain. She was no holds barred stubborn about wanting to stay home. She said dying was strange enough without doing it in a strange place with strangers.

My mom is an ICU nurse so home is where she stayed. Her room had pink and white striped wallpaper and a ceiling with stars on it that glowed in the dark. She had every album Taylor Swift ever made, and they played all day. She said Taylor Swift was going to sing her out.

We have two dachshunds named Lucy in the Sky and Imagine, and those dogs would get up on that bed with her and snuggle right close until she went to sleep at night. She told me not to be sad because she'd had a really good time every day of her life not counting the last two weeks. She didn't feel like talking too much, but she wanted us to. She said she was holding on to our voices. She said the words were keeping her with us as long as possible before she left on her journey.

So Mom and Dad and me and Grandma, who was staying with us, just kept the words going and didn't let the silence in. Mom stayed in there with her all night sitting in a rocking chair Grandpa had made. She had us all write messages to her on her sheets that she could take with her on her travels. We each wrote one every day.

I remember on her last Wednesday, I asked her how she was doing, and she said she had finished packing her bags. She said she was sorry for the trouble, but I had to live two lives now because she was leaving me hers. When she was gone, the two dachshunds howled. So did I, but I did it inside where you couldn't hear it. There is more to silence than you think.

The Swimmer

By F. Xavier Hogan

About the play: A young man at a corner bus stop is absolutely convinced he is drowning though there is no water in the vicinity. Each person who passes by becomes somehow involved in the situation, but each is more interested in promoting their own point of view than helping the man. This existential one-act builds to a climax in which the young man dies, yet his death has no emotional impact upon those around him.

Time period: 1973.

Young Man
Late teens

About the scene: The Swimmer has just finished speaking with a drunk when another young man comes along and converses with The Swimmer about the situation.

Young Man:

Hey, that guy was really something, wasn't he? Wow, drunks are such loose people. That guy was beautiful, wasn't he? I mean, it takes so much endurance to be a drunk. Day in and day out. It really takes dedication, you know. Hey, are you sick or something? Are you alright? Can you talk? Wow, you're a mute, aren't you? That's really something, I never met a mute before. What an experience. I mean, I'm really beside myself. You can't talk. […]

You can talk. Wow! […]

You can't swim? Well, just jump in the water and pretend. You can do it. Kick your legs and paddle with your arms. It's simple. […]

No, you won't, as long as you keep kicking you won't drown. It's just like that drunk. If you want to be a drunk you've got to keep drinking and to swim you've got to keep kicking. [...]

Wow, you're a pessimist. I mean, I can feel the depression all around you. You're really down, aren't you? Wow, that's crazy. There's no reason for it. Just because you can't swim? You can swim. And suppose you can't? You can, but suppose you can't? All you have to do is stay out of the water. Build a bridge or something, walk around the water. Hey, it's not so bad. Swimming isn't everything, you know. Unless you fall out of a boat or something, then it might come in handy, but like I say, just keep kicking and you'll be all right. You might even surprise yourself. Here, have a cigarette. [...]

Wow, you don't smoke and you don't drink and you're still depressed. You should feel great not using anything. Is it just depression or is it something bigger? Do you... are you mentally ill or something? Because if you are, don't let it bother you because everybody else is in the same boat. Everything's crazy nowadays. You know what I heard the other day? They found a cure for cancer. Really! Front page headlines... in red yet! Cure for cancer! Everybody feels better now. Just think, we don't have to worry about dying of cancer anymore. Isn't that fantastic? But when you're depressed, even the good things don't make any difference unless, of course, you've got cancer. Is that it? Are you dying of cancer? If you are, don't worry about it. They found the cure.

Is it a girl? There's plenty of girls around, or guys, if that's it. You can have a different one every night. Grow your hair long if you want. That's cool now, too. I mean, you can get the girls with long hair and still hold down a job. Even my parents think long hair's okay. My dad's getting a little curly in the back, you know. And you're young, you've got a long life ahead of you. Just think, you'll be able to go to the moon before you die. They'll have charter flights to the moon, and with the new regulations, you won't have to be a member of a charter group to take advantage of it. It's not going to happen tomorrow or the next day, but it's still something to look forward to. The moon, it's so far away and so mysterious and you'll be able to sit on it. Imagine, sitting on the moon looking down on Earth wondering what everybody's doing. It'll be crazy, don't you think?

A Tale of Two Cities

Adapted by Joellen K. Bland

About the play: Set in France and England at the time of the French Revolution, this faithful adaptation utilizes four narrators along with an ensemble of performers to cover all the main points of the classic story by Charles Dickens.

Time period: 1790s.

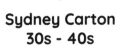

Sydney Carton
30s - 40s

About the scene: Charles Darnay is sentenced to death for returning to Paris. The revolution has destroyed the country, and everything has become a crime worthy of death by the guillotine. However, Carton, a longtime friend of the family with an uncanny resemblance to Darnay, has decided to trade places with Darnay. Carton sneaks Darnay out of the prison and takes his place on death row. As he is being placed in the guillotine, Carton speaks his final, famous words.

Carton:

I see the lives for which I lay down my life, in days to come, peaceful, prosperous, and happy in that England I shall see no more. I see Lucie with a child upon her bosom who bears my name. I see her father, aged and bent, but otherwise restored and faithful to all men in his healing office and at peace. I see the good old man of business, so long their friend, in ten years' time enriching them with all he has and passing tranquilly to his reward. I see that I hold a sanctuary in their hearts and in the hearts of their descendants, generations hence. It is a far, far better thing that I do than I have ever done. It is a far, far better rest I go to than I have ever known. *(He kneels and bends his head forward.)*

Tested

By Kendra Thomas

About the play: Standardized testing is all about rules and protocol. Two #2 pencils. Sanctioned calculators. Carefully filled-out Scantrons. But is standardized testing really fair when the students themselves are anything but "standard"? Sure, for some it's no big deal — testing is just a chance to earn ice cream or cash rewards from their parents when they do well. But then there are those with dyslexia, test anxiety, ADHD — as the students hit the panic button, it takes their caring teacher to remind and reassure the class that each of them is far more than just a test score.

Time period: The present.

Will
Teens

About the scene: Will delivers his monologue to the audience, revealing his struggles with ADHD and how it makes testing difficult for him.

Will:

Yeah. Relax? How am I supposed to relax?

Sometimes I sit on my hands... but then I realize I can't actually bubble in answers if I'm sitting on my hands. So then I tap my pencil. But then I see the teacher coming. Even though I have small-group testing, there's other students, and I can't do anything to distract them. So I stop.

Then I just chew on the end of the pencil. Last test, I chewed the eraser off! It was the school's pencil, too, and the teacher monitoring the test was so irritated.

And if there's windows, I find myself staring out them. Just staring. I start imagining what's happening outside, thinking about lunch… the test just fades away! Ten minutes later, I haven't answered a single question.

ADHD—I've had it since… well, I've had it forever, but they told my parents I had it three years ago. Do you know what it's like to sit still when you've got ADHD? It's torture! You're just sitting there, in a quiet little box, and you can't move. You can't talk, and all your body and mouth want to do is move.

Have you ever had that restless leg thing? You know, where there are these little tingly vibrations in your leg, and you just feel the urge to move it? I've had that, and ADHD is like that. Only, that vibration? It's constant, and it's all over. A little twitch that makes your whole body just want to move.

Imagine taking a test like that! Just imagine…

A Thing of Beauty

By Maurice Berger

About the play: A gentle old man enters a park carrying a piece of beautifully formed driftwood, hoping others will thrill to its beauty as he does. The reactions to the driftwood are as varied as the people he encounters. But in their reactions, the characters display their true natures, and in revealing their attitudes toward the driftwood, they draw a fascinating picture of life itself.

Time period: 1960s.

Jones
20s - 40s

About the scene: The old man has just been harassed by a policeman, who scolded him for littering, citing the different fines he could assess. After the policeman leaves, Jones, a businessman, arrives to eat lunch at the park. Jones explains to the old man his opinion about the police force's authority and draws a parallel to his boss in the corporate world.

Jones:

They got to cause you trouble. Makes 'em feel important. They can't just leave a guy alone. [...]

They think they know everything. Put the thing back out there if you want to. You're not going to sell it holding it like that. That cop won't be back for maybe an hour. You just put the thing back and show him he can't push you around. [...]

You can't let those guys push you around or they'll run all over you. [...]

We got murderers running the streets, and he rousts someone around about a crummy piece of wood. You give a guy a little power and they're all alike. Take my boss down at the office. He'd be pushing me around if I let him, but a guy has his self-respect. Like I start bringing this briefcase to the office and then taking it out with me at noon. I can see the boss burning to know what I got in the bag. One day he looks like he thinks maybe I'm selling something on the side and the next day he stares at me like I'm smuggling out all his paperclips. Boy, it burns him. I'm not going to give him the satisfaction of knowing what is in the bag, though, because that would be letting him push me around. Get it?

The Thirty-Three Little Pigs
By Brian D. Taylor

About this play: In this predator-vs.-prey send-up, the thirty-three pigs in the meadow continuously outsmart the hungry wolf, much in the style of Roadrunner and Coyote or Tom and Jerry. From Straw, Stick, and Brick pigs to Pirate, Chef, and Ninja pigs (plus 27 others!), they each have their chance to misdirect, heckle, and hound the bumbling Big Bad Wolf, who only finds himself further and further from getting his fill of little piggies!

Time period: Once upon a time...

Bunker Pig
Ageless

About the scene: The Big Bad Wolf is roaming the meadow, trying to catch one of the dozens of pigs who lives there. Bunker Pig, however, lives safely underground and tells the audience why that's the better choice when there's a dangerous wolf around.

Bunker Pig:

(Slurps a spoonful of corn straight from the can.) Ya heard the news about that wolf, too, eh? Yeah, it's bad news alright. Bad, bad news! Lucky for me, I saw all this comin' long ago, and I'm prepared!

All them other pigs thought I was a fool for buildin' this underground bunker. But who's havin' the last laugh now? All of them other pigs think they're safe, but they're foolin' themselves up there in that sunny meadow. I saw the dark times ahead. I knew what was comin'. And nothing's going to harm me down here! Not some ol' mangy wolf, that's for sure!

Them other pigs up there...? They don't know! I've been preparing for dark times like these for years. And I'll be safe down here while the rest of them are in grave danger. See, I've got three years of rations down here in my bunker. Got me some canned corn here. *(Takes a bite.)* Let's see what else... *(Grabs cans.)* Here's some canned grits, canned slop, canned squash, and—ooh, my favorite!—canned candy apples!

Them other pigs? They've just been eatin' and sleepin' and rollin' around in the mud and sun all this time without a worry in the world. I tried to tell them. "We've got to be prepared for the worst, folks!" Yeah, they'd make fun of me for planning for the end of times. But who's laughing now, huh? Sure, they call me a worrywart and a conspiracy theorist. They've even called me... *(Gestures with air quotes.)* ..."The Ground Hog." That's right. The Ground Hog. But I'll tell you what. I'll wear that name like a badge of honor, because it means I outsmarted all of them fools and planned ahead. I didn't build no house of straw or sticks or bricks. Nah, all of those have security problems.

It's true! Even that brick house! Don't believe me? Two words— *(Counts out each syllable as a separate word.)* —chim-ney. And that's why I built my home here deep underground. Totally secure, off the grid, off the radar. Yeah, I'll wear that moniker as a badge of honor, alright. I am... the Ground Hog! And I have nothing to be afraid of down here! *(Slurps another spoonful of corn.)*

◆◆◆

The Time Machine
By Tim Kelly

About the play: Young Filby, the inventor, invites some scientists to his home to hear about his latest invention, a machine that travels through time. When the guests return a week later, Filby relays to them the story of his travel into the future, from which he has just returned. Accompanied by his cook, Mrs. Watchett, they tell of meeting the Eloi, a strange race of young people, and the Morlock, a brutal race that lives beneath the Earth's surface. When the Morlocks steal the time machine, Mrs. Watchett and Filby must enter the dark tunnels underground to get it back. They are lucky to escape with their lives, yet are met with nothing but skepticism and mockery when they return to the late 1800s. As Mrs. Watchett defends the retelling of their adventures as factual, Filby climbs into the time machine and disappears once again.

Time period: 1895 to the distant future.

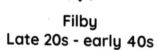

Filby
Late 20s - early 40s

About the scene: Up to this point, no one believes in Filby's time machine. Filby knows other greats have gone before, just to be written off as mad. He is getting ready to prove the skeptics wrong. In this monologue, Filby steps into the time machine and narrates the dizzying sensation of time travel, culminating in an abrupt halt when he has finally reached his destination.

Filby:

They want proof, they shall have proof. (*Seats himself in the machine.*) The question is… to the past, or to the future? The future, I think. (*Slowly pushes forward on a lever. A spotlight strikes to the right of the time machine. Filby gets out of the seat, steps into the light, and continues his narration.*)

I seemed to reel; I felt a nightmare sensation of falling. Looking 'round, I saw that the time machine had, somehow, got itself back into the workshop. I drew a breath and set my teeth. The workshop got hazy and went dark. I am afraid I cannot convey the peculiar sensations of time traveling. They are unpleasant... I saw the moon spinning swiftly through her quarters from new to full, and had a faint glimpse of circling stars... there was a clap of thunder in my ears as I hurdled far into the future wondering what year I was passing through... I heard a great hissing sound... I thought my head would explode... and, then, another terrible crack of thunder and I realized the time machine was coming to an abrupt stop! [...]

Suddenly, there was nothing but eternal night! *(The crash has thrown him off. Filby is on the ground, several feet from the time machine. Coming to.)* Ow... ow... ow... *(Sits up, rubs his head.)* My head, my poor head. Ow... ow... ow...

Tuckered

By Matthew K. Begbie

About the play: Prince Willop is no Sleeping Beauty. In fact, he can't catch a single wink! Cursed at birth never to slumber, the young prince longs to live a normal life. Instead, Willop sits. Willop reads. Willop watches out the window. And Willop daydreams of leaving the tower where King Duncan and Queen Cordelia have kept him locked up for nearly 16 years to protect him from other wicked afflictions out in the world. Exhausted court caretaker and Willop's only friend, Stewart the Steward, would love to finally get a good night's rest himself, so he ventures out of the kingdom to find a way to break the curse.

Time period: Once upon a time…

Prince Willop
16 years old

About the scene: On the morning of his sixteenth birthday, Prince Willop complains to Steward of the lengths of his boredom.

Prince Willop:

Steward! Steward, I'm bored! I'm so bored I think I'm losing my mind! If I don't find something to do… I– I– I think I'll die!

(Starts digging through his things, rummaging through books and rifling through knickknacks, seemingly unsure of what he's looking for.) I've done everything I can possibly imagine to do! *(As he begins to go over all his various studies, he hands Stewart various books, piling them high as he continues.)* I've studied everything from anthropology to zoology. Every animal from aardvarks to zebras! Every tree from alders to yews! I've left no stone unturned in geology—from argillite to wackestone! I've read the dictionary—twice. *(Adds a dictionary to the pile.)* And I've pored over, studied, and skimmed

through the thesaurus—thrice! *(Throws a thesaurus on the stack.)* I've assessed antediluvian albums, buried myself in Byzantine books, charted cautious courses, decoded decrepit documents, examined enigmatic and excursive encyclopedias, found nothing fun, frankly, about forestry—I've garnered a gargantuan gallery of guides, honed my historiography, ingested intricate inscriptions, jotted in jumbled journals, and even kept a key of kaleidoscopic keepsakes! I've learned lost languages and mastered mathematics! I've nitpicked nuanced novels, overcome oratorical obstacles, perfected precise painting, and quelled the most quizzing of quandaries! I've read rambling reports, studied the stars and the seas, trained in timeworn transcription tactics, unraveled the unsolved, vanquished the vexing, wearily re-wrote weatherworn wisdoms, and—And I have zero things left to learn!

Two Fronts

By Christy Fredrickson

About the play: Two Fronts explores the two sides of World War II—the war front and the home front. The men elude death on the front lines while the women work in the factories to keep them going. This powerful one act is an emotional look into the harrowing stories of a generation of families torn apart by war.

Time period: 1942.

Thompson
40s

About the scene: Thompson had tried to enlist in the army but was turned away because of his wooden leg. If given the choice, he would be on the front lines of battle. Instead, he is working as a factory supervisor to do what he can for the war effort on the home front. A young man named Fred had enlisted with his brother, but his brother recently died in training before they even made it to the war front. Terrified of also ending up dead, Fred now wants to desert. Thompson is outraged as Fred reveals his plan and is determined to knock some sense into him about what it means to serve your country. He has just punched Fred and knocked him to the floor.

Thompson:

Now, you listen to me, you sorry little weasel. You're going back. You're going back to your unit, and you're going to stay there. You're going to do your duty like a man. Everybody is scared. Everybody! But you're going to do your duty, because that's what a man does even when he's scared. You understand me? […]

You see this bum leg? It's wood. I lost it in France in the first war. I tried to join up, but they wouldn't let me. […]

You wanted sympathy? Okay, I'll give you sympathy. I will give you one hour to get back to the base, then I'm calling them. If you're back, I won't say a thing. If you're still gone, I'll tell them you've deserted, and they'll find you and hang you.

I know you're scared, son. We all are. It doesn't matter. Your brother wouldn't want you to skip out, would he? Do the right thing. Go on back. Being scared won't last forever. Being a deserter will. Come on.

The Waiting Room

By Noah Bennett

About the play: In a simple waiting room, people arrive at their appointed time to face the unknown of what lies beyond an ominous closed door. Earl Trent, an older man, arrives early and is instructed by the businesslike receptionist to wait till his time. Scared about why he was summoned to the waiting room, he encounters people of all ages arriving at their assigned time. From all walks of life, each person he meets has followed a unique journey to get to this moment... their time to die. Some never saw it coming, others knew all too well that their time was coming, and a few even welcomed it. Through his encounters with the others in the waiting room, Earl gains both insight and courage about the meaning of life.

Time period: The present.

Robin
50s

About the scene: On the surface, Robin is lighthearted and fun. In fact, his manic quality is quite reminiscent of Robin Williams. Unlike the others in the waiting room, however, he has not received a telegram about an appointment. When he is refused entry, he is impatient with the receptionist, creating a big fuss that reveals his underlying sense of despair. Yes, Robin is aware that the appointments are for death, and he wants one.

Robin:

(Jumps to his feet, shocked.) What is this about? You let the beautiful women go right ahead, but *(Indicates Earl.)* not a sick man who needs it! Meanwhile, I'm here, and I wait, and I wait, and I wait, only to be told to come back another time. *(In an operator voice.)* "Please hold, sir, your call is very important to us!" And when I do wait—wait for that agonizing limitless amount of infinity—guess what happens? Guess what happens,

Captain Smiles? *(Receptionist does not respond.)* I wait some more! And it's at that point I realize, I haven't lived a life. I've waited a life. And for what? This? Where do I go next? Where are we now? What is this place?! What is the point in these telegrams? *(Grabs Earl's telegram and reads.)* "Dear Earl Trent, you are requested by the highest authority to report to the Mapplethorpe Building in the downtown district on September 28 at exactly 1:14 pm. Please bring your most current form of identification." That's it. That's all they tell you. They pull people away from their lives, so they can live a life of waiting!

Oh, that's right. Some get to go right on in, like they were given a fast pass in life. But that's all life is, it's waiting. It's waiting for the next thing, which is more waiting. Everyone grows up basking in innocence and loathing in adolescence, thinking that we live in a big, great world and that anything's possible. "Oh, if you don't like the world, you can change it." Buzz! Wrong! No, you can't change the world. We all just have "appointments." We're all just another wave in the sea, getting a little bit older. The teenage years, where your mindset is to rebel against everything you've ever known, because you have the world by the tail! The truth is, no one has any idea what's going on! Life is one big mess! *(Slams his hands on the receptionist's desk.)* Life is one big disaster, like this place!

(Moves away from desk.) Why is it such a mess in here?! This place is a mess, life is a mess!

(Comes to a sobering realization.) I'm a mess. Earl, I have a question. If God is real, then why are we forced to wait, to suffer?

◆◆◆

Judge
Late 60s - early 80s

About the scene: Judge is waiting a few seats away from Earl, who senses that the elderly man is wise and true. Meanwhile, Judge immediately senses that Earl is scared of what is on the other side of the door. Earl and Judge strike up a conversation. Judge tries to ease Earl's anxiety while sharing his own thoughts about life and death from his experience on the bench.

Judge:

Scared? I know that feeling. I think everyone knows that feeling all too well. It's a deceptive feeling. Is the grass greener on the other side? We can never know for sure, but every human being has a fascinating ability to sense the truth. The right in a situation. A gut instinct, you may call it. The best part of a gut instinct is that no matter how much you convince your mind of the other, the gut knows what's right.

As a judge you have to make some really tough calls sometimes. At times, you don't even want to, but the law makes you. There is only one law, Earl. One time, I had to decide whether or not to sentence a man to death or not. To this day, it was the hardest decision I ever had to make.

Well, the facts were there. This man was guilty beyond a shadow of a doubt. He was guilty of a dehumanizing crime, and it made me sick to see the victim's family so broken by what this man had done. After being found guilty, it was time to do my job, to give him a sentence. Life in prison or death? Immediately my mind went to death, because in a situation like that, it seems like the only way to provide justice. But then I thought for a moment and asked myself, "What makes his life any less valuable than yours?" On the other hand, there are things from that hearing I will never be able to wipe from my mind. That girl's mother crying and screaming as she had to relive the horror of those events in the courtroom, the jury members with pale ghostly faces as the facts of the case began to surface, the defense attorney wiping the sweat off his forehead as he tried to defend this beast. But the worst of it all was the look on this monster's face. You could tell he didn't regret a single thing that he had done. I wanted to give this man a second chance so badly, but sometimes life doesn't give you a second chance, Earl, and that's the reality of it. I remember the crack in my voice as I declared this man's fate to the members of the courtroom. I will never forget that day.

Walkin' Home

By Steven Orth

About the play: Sonja was a rebellious child who left home at the age of 17. Ever since then, her father has stared out the window, waiting for her to return. After a two-year downward spiral, she now stands on her old front porch, contemplating her decision to walk through the door again. Her travel companion, Stan, attempts to dissuade her from returning by reminding her why she left in the first place. Meanwhile, inside the house, her parents, George and Jenny, and her older sister, Nora, are preparing Thanksgiving dinner. Through flashbacks, the audience learns the struggles they all have had both before and after Sonja left. The story ends as Sonja walks through the door with the hope of a different, better relationship with her mother, father, and sister—one for which they, too, have been yearning.

Time period: The present.

Past George
40s

About the scene: In this monologue, we see a reenactment of the day Sonja left home for good. George tells her how much she is appreciated and loved in their home, but Sonja refuses to listen.

Past George:

Sonja, do you believe that your mother and I love you? […]

I think you do.

Think back on everything that's happened in this house. I remember carrying you home from the hospital. I was so excited that I made your mother drive the car. I didn't even put you in the car seat. When we rolled into the driveway, I took you around and "introduced" you to each of our neighbors. I was so proud. Your grandparents used to warn me that I would create a monster if I never let you sleep in your crib. I always had a difficult time letting you go.

When you were two and scraped your knee on the curb, Nora came tearing into the house yelling for me. Even she believed that I could take away your pain. I know that was impossible, but I so wanted to make it your reality—that Daddy would always be there to make you feel better. *(Past Sonja rolls her eyes and turns away.)* What? Don't believe that your "evil" sister cares about you? [...]

I also recall a three-year-old bursting at the seams to be a "big sister." After you were born, it was more of the same. When your mother or I would wake up in the middle of the night to check on you, there she'd be, standing guard over your crib, telling me to be quiet and not disturb her baby. Every meal, she wanted to spoon the carrots and squash into your mouth. She wouldn't eat a thing until she knew you were full. [...]

(Crosses to the front door and opens it. Puts the key under the rock by the door.) The key will always be here for you under this rock. You will always be welcome here. This is your home.

Stan
20s

About the scene: Down on her luck because her quest for fame and fortune has proven fruitless, Sonja stands on the porch with her friend Stan, contemplating returning home. Sonja has just claimed that she never asked her father or anyone for help. Stan is insulted by this comment and feels dejected that she would so quickly cast him aside.

Stan:

"I never asked him, or anyone, for anything." That's not entirely true, is it? [...]

You've asked me for lots of things. You asked for my help with your grades, right? You wanted something to help you stay awake later so you could do your homework. I let you know where to get pills. You wanted to find out if there was any way to get the answers before the test. I showed you who to buy the keys from. You asked if there was a way to get As and Bs on your papers without writing them. I pointed out the websites where you could download your essays from the internet. Long story short—you asked for my help, and you got it every time. [...]

You're right. You don't owe me a thing. No gratitude whatsoever. We'll just conveniently forget whose idea it was to light it out of here when things got so bad. Who went with you every step of the way? Let's ignore that, too. Heck, let's just forget the last two years ever happened! [...]

But you can't. What's done is done. No amount of wishing can change anything.

◆◆◆

The Wall

By Richard Lauchman

About the play: It is shortly before dawn on the morning of the crucifixion. The two thieves of legend, Dimas and Gestas, wait in their cell. Gestas waits calmly, calling up scraps from his past, hoping to blot out the sound of soldiers erecting the crosses. Dimas gazes through the window at the sweep of stars, worrying about the impending pain and wondering what death will be like. Through a small hole in the wall they can glimpse the other person awaiting crucifixion, the person about whom enormous tales have been told. As the thieves await the dawn, they contemplate the stranger who perhaps could save their souls.

Time period: About 30 AD.

Gestas
30s

About the scene: This monologue opens the play, with Gestas in a relaxed, supine position, hands cupped behind his head and staring at the ceiling, lost in pleasant recollections. His demeanor is in distinct contrast to Dimas's, whose only thoughts are of his impending crucifixion the next day.

Gestas:

No, you can say what you like about cheese. I'll take roast lamb any day. *(With relish.)* With a little pepper.

(Sigh. Nostalgically.) I remember one time—oh, years back, it was. I couldn't have been more than a whelp. Got myself lost in the hills. On my way from one shithole to another, I don't know. Back then it was easy to get lost in those hills. *(Observantly.)* It still is. *(Brief pause, meditatively.)* But I remember I was hungry that night, boy. Hungry as a lion, let

me tell you. Hadn't had a thing in days. *(Realistic tone.)* Oh, you know, a few figs now and then, bread when I could steal it, but I mean—I mean, that's not enough for a man. A man needs meat. A man like me. He needs his meat. Anyway, there I was, walking over the stones, belly full of wind. I swear I could feel it—flopping, like flopping around inside of me. Against my ribs, you know what I mean? I could feel it flopping against my ribs. I was ready to eat anything. Anything.

And that's when I smelled it. Roast lamb! *(Sighs.)* I thought at first I was crazy. I thought I was crazy from being so hungry. But I kept on going and the smell got stronger. Then I saw a fire a little ways off. Then I knew I wasn't crazy. Somebody was roasting a lamb.

(Quietly.) I came up real quiet-like and hid myself behind a rock. *(Laughs.)* I remember my stomach was growling so loud I thought sure he'd hear it. *(Sarcastically.)* But he didn't hear it. No, he was sitting by the fire, all wrapped up in his cloak, working on his wine. *(Peremptory snort.)* You know how he drank? You know how shepherds drink? See, they take a goat belly and put their wine in it. And then they hold it up over their head and aim the prick at their mouth and squirt the wine out through the prick into their mouth. Wasteful as all hell! *(Laughs.)* He was missing his mouth, he was hitting himself on the nose, on the chin, everywhere but in his mouth, I mean I could see it dripping off his beard. But did he care? Shit, you think he cared? Nah, he didn't care.

I mean, he figured he was only going to piss it anyway, so why should he care?

(Sighs profoundly.) Meanwhile, on this spit over the fire, just oozing juice, was the prettiest little lamb you'd ever want to

see. *(Shuts eyes, groans in recollected ecstasy.)* Ah, the aroma! I can almost... I mean, even now, I can almost... *(Licks his lips, opens his eyes.)*

Mind you, this was a shepherd. Eating his own sheep, can you beat that? He's supposed to be watching out for 'em and he goes and eats 'em! *(Snorts vehemently.)* His own sheep! *(Closes his eyes and smiles.)* Ah, but didn't she sizzle, though! You should have seen her sizzle. Bright drops of lamb fat in the bright fire. *(Sighs. Opens his eyes. Angrily.)* But he wasn't turning her, you know? He wasn't even turning her. Underneath she was starting to go all black. He wasn't even turning her! When I saw that— let me tell you, when I saw that... *(Laughs darkly.)* Anyway, I cracked his skull in short order. *(Throws a series of wild punches into space.)* Pow! Pow! Pow! No, I'll take roast lamb any day. You can have your cheese. I never cared much for cheese.

Just give me my roast lamb. With a little pepper.

Why Darkness Seems So Light

By Helen Frost and Harvey Cocks

About the play: Here is a chilling look at the violence that pervades teenagers' lives, regardless of their social status or upbringing. Based on the writings of 250 high school students, the play is a stirring series of linked scenes depicting the effects of violence on young people, their families, and others around them. While the topic is heavy and intended for mature audiences, the play is not depressing. It introduces a sense of hope that the love of parents, siblings, friends, and teachers can help teens through experiences of violence and rough times.

Time period: The present.

Nathan
Teens

About the scene: Nathan is what most people would call a good kid. He comes from a troubled home, yet maintains a close relationship with his brother and mom. Unfortunately, his stepfather, Ralph, runs their household with physical force. Nathan's last gift from his real father was his dog, Scarlett, but Ralph killed Scarlett for barking too much. Nathan is beside himself with grief, totally heartbroken.

Nathan:

(Runs onstage and falls to his knees, gun in hand. He attempts to catch his breath.) I loved that little dog more than anyone. Scarlett never asked for anything. Just someone to scratch her back... feed her. I could have a rotten day, and she'd see me and come running to me, making those little happy sounds. She'd look at me with those big eyes, and nothing seemed so bad anymore. Oh, God, I'm going to miss her! *(Sudden sob, covers his face, then looks up.)*

Why did you do it, Ralph? Not "Dad"! You're not my father! I hate you!

(Looks down at the gun, pauses, then speaks in a quiet voice.) I should've killed him. *(Another pause, looking at the gun, thinking.)* What's the use? What's the use of anything? Nothing's ever gonna get better. I'm tired of fighting everyone.

(Holds up the gun, looks at it for a moment, then looks upward.) I know it's not right. Preacher Davis says so and Mom would too. I know all that... but, I just can't... Mom, please forgive me. I don't mean to hurt you... I just can't... *(Raises gun, holds it out, pointed at himself.)*

Yearbook

By Steven Fendrich

About the play: Four high school students are sneaking a peak at this year's yearbook. As they scroll through the pages and comment on the pictures, flashback scenes come to life onstage, telling the story behind each image. Through these vignettes, the students come to have a better understanding of one another, realizing that none of them fits neatly into any of the high school stereotypes with which they are so often associated.

Time period: The present.

Tim
16 - 18

About the scene: Tim is the star of his high school basketball team. He relives the final moments of the state championship game, a game he always dreamed of to make his dad proud.

Tim:

I'll see you after the game, Dad. *(To audience.)* And what a game it was. I swear the score went back and forth a million times. I had to play up against this one guy who must have been six inches taller than me. This guy was big... and strong! I can remember how exhausted I was just guarding this guy. Man, what a game! It sure went fast! It seems every time I would blink, a quarter would be over. And even though I thought we should have been up by twenty, the score was always even. But Coach kept me in because I had a hot hand that night. I mean, that was truly my night! I was able to get off some good shots... and the lucky ones were falling in, too. But the Panthers were doing great. Every shot we would make, they would come back and match it. When they went up by one with just five seconds left, we called timeout. The plan was for me to get the ball and go to the basket. So, as soon as I touched the ball, I took it fast to the hoop. *(Runs toward "basket.")* I went up and the big guy hit me on the arm. With the place screaming, I didn't even hear a whistle. I sort of remember the cheers, I guess. All I know is that my head was spinning. The ref handed me the ball and told me I had two shots. The other team called a timeout just to get my mind working too much. But Coach was great. He had confidence in me, and I believed him. This was my time. You know, the minutes of fame everyone always talks about. My teammates were yelling and slapping me on the back. Yeah, my head was spinning. But after all, I was the best shooter on my team, and like Dad said, I'd been carrying my team. Who could doubt that this was the moment I'd been waiting for all my life? You see, this was living the dream. When you grow up being a jock like me, you dream of hitting the homerun in the bottom of the ninth to win the World Series, catching the touchdown pass to win the Super Bowl or...

...sinking the shot to win the state championship. I was actually living my dream! So I knew I would win it all. I stepped up to the foul line.... *(Bounces ball three times and looks at "basket," ready to shoot.)* I wiped off the sweat that was dripping from my forehead. *(Wipes forehead.)* I bounced the ball three times. You see, I always bounce the ball three times before a foul shot.

Okay. This is it. This is fame. In a few seconds I'll be cutting the net. Fans will be mauling me, carrying me off of the court.

And Dad.

So I took a deep breath. *(Deep breath.)* And shot. Okay. Okay. Okay. No problem. I'll send it into overtime and then win it for the team. But what did I just do wrong? My dream is out-of-sync. There are my teammates. *(Looks upstage.)* They're so nervous they can't even look up. Okay. Let's just send it into overtime. Three times. *(Bounces ball three times.)* Deep breath. *(Takes breath.)* And... I can't believe it! *(Falls to the ground and pounds his fist on the floor.)* I blew it! I blew it! I blew it! *(Continues to pound his fist as his dad approaches.)* And there's Dad. I don't want to look him in the eyes. Wasn't this his moment, too? Isn't this what a father dreams about? What he tells his friends about for years to come? And now I have to face him. I've let him down. *(Looks up at his dad.)* I screwed up, Dad. I blew it. I missed it. I'm sorry. Really. I'm sorry.

Appendix A
Monologues by Tone
◆◆◆
Comedic Monologues (C)

Play	Character	Age	Year
Alien Invasion!	Bridger	50s-60s	Present
Bayou	Tooney	Early teens	Present
The Best Worst Day of My Life	Mr. Ridge	30s-40s	Present
Bigger Than Life	Pecos Bill	Mid 20s-50s	Early 1900s
Black and Blue Friday	Bubba	Teens	Present
The Boy Who Cried Werewolf	Chris	Early teens	Present
The Canterbury Tales	Chanticleer	Ageless	1300s
Disorder in the Court	Scammerton	30s-40s	Present
	Glen	20s-30s	
Dr. Evil and the Pigeons with Lasers	Dr. Evil	Late 20s	Present
In the Hood	Guy Jantic	40s or older	Present
Love at First Thought	Norm [1]	Late teens-early 20s	Present
The Most Viewed Least Watched Talk Show in History	Quinn	20s	Present
The Nose That Ran Away from Its Face	Nose	Ageless	Timeless
	Boy	Teens	
Paul Bunyan and the Hard Winter	Rip Snortin' Sam	Late 20s-early 50s	1891
Playground	Big John	20 years old	1984
Rememberin' Stuff	David	Teens	Present
	Pete		
Shakespeare by Monkeys	Riley	20s-30s	Present
Sir Huey and the Dragon	Dragon	Ageless	Once upon a time

Play	Character	Age	Year
The Thirty-Three Little Pigs	Bunker Pig	Ageless	Once upon a time
Tuckered	Prince Willop	16 years old	Once upon a time

Seriocomic Monologues (S)

Play	Character	Age	Year
The Adventures of Rikki Tikki Tavi	Puran Bhagat	Late 60s or older	Late 1800s
A Bowl of Soup	Oscar	Late teens-early 20s	Present
Cirrius, Nebraska	The Stranger	30s	Present
The Great Gatsby	Gatsby [1]	32 years old	1922
If These Walls Could Talk	Stanley	Teens	Present
The Last Leaf	Old Behrman	73 years old	1907
Legend of Sleepy Hollow	Brom Bones	20s	Early 1800s
Little Women	Laurie	20s -30s	1860s
	Professor Bhaer	Late 30s-early 40s	
Love at First Thought	Norm [2]	Late teens-early 20s	Present
Mayfair Lady	Higgins	40s	1912
	Doolittle	40s or older	
Pollyanna	Jimmy Bean	10 years old	1910
Pride and Prejudice	Mr. Darcy	20s-30s	Early 1800s
Quaran-Teens	Josh	16-18	2020

Dramatic Monologues (D)

Play	Character	Age	Year
Always Bella	Bart	Teens	Present
Amelia, Once More	Alphonse	40s or older	Present
	Tom	20s or older	
Bang! Bang! You're Dead	Actor #3	15 years old	Present
The Boy with No Name	Allen	40s	Present
	Eddy	18 years old	
A Child Went Forth	Boy	Late teens	Present
Dracula	Van Helsing	Mid 40s-early 60s	1890s
	Harker	Late 20s-early 40s	
The Empty Chair	Speaker #5	Teens	Present
Fosters	Petey	Older dog	Present
Frankenstein	Dr. Victor Frankenstein	20s-30s	1816
	The Creature [1]	Ageless	
	The Creature [2]		
Gossip	Andy	Teens	Present
The Great Gatsby	Nick	30 years old	1922
	Gatsby [2]	32 years old	
Jim Bridger—Mountain Man	Jim Bridger	60s	1860s
Lover's Leap	Reporter	Late 40s-50s	Late 1970s
May I Have Your Attention, Please?	Chris	15 years old	Present

Dramatic monologues cont.

Play	Character	Age	Year
Memory Garden	Dan	Late 30s-early 40s	Present
Poe: Dreams of Madness	Edgar Allan Poe	30s	1840s
Rememberin' Stuff	Billy	Teens	Present
	Tony	18 years old	
The Reunion	Ali	Late 50s	2021
The Scarlet Letter	Arthur Dimmesdale	Mid 30s or older	1700s
Scheherazade	Grand Vizier	40s or older	700 BC
Struggling for the Surface	Joe	40s	Present
	James	30s	
Stuck	Unnamed	Teens	2020
The Swimmer	Young Man	Late teens	1973
A Tale of Two Cities	Carton	30s-40s	1790s
Tested	Will	Teens	Present
A Thing of Beauty	Jones	20s-40s	1960s
The Time Machine	Filby	Late 20s-early 40s	1895 to future
Two Fronts	Thompson	40s	1942
Waiting Room	Robin	50s	Present
	Judge	Late 60s-early 80s	
Walkin' Home	Past George	40s	Present
	Stan	20s	
Wall, The	Gestas	30s	30 AD
Why Darkness Seems So Light	Nathan	Teens	Present
Yearbook	Tim	16-18	Present

◆◆◆

Appendix B
Monologues by Time Period
◆◆◆

Year	Play	Character	Age	Tone
Once upon a time	*Sir Huey and the Dragon*	Dragon	Ageless	C
	The Thirty-Three Little Pigs	Bunker Pig	Ageless	C
	Tuckered	Prince Willop	16 years old	C
700 BC	*Scheherazade*	Grand Vizier	40s or older	D
30 AD	*The Wall*	Gestas	30s	D
1300s	*The Canterbury Tales*	Chanticleer	Ageless	C
1700s	*The Scarlet Letter*	Arthur Dimmesdale	Mid 30s or older	D
1790s	*A Tale of Two Cities*	Carton	30s - 40s	D
Early 1800s	*Legend of Sleepy Hollow*	Brom Bones	20s	S
	Pride and Prejudice	Mr. Darcy	20s - 30s	S
1816	*Frankenstein*	Dr. Victor Frankenstein	20S - 30S	D
		The Creature [1]	Ageless	D
		The Creature [2]		D
1840s	*Poe: Dreams of Madness*	Edgar Allan Poe	30s	D
1860s	*Jim Bridger—Mountain Man*	Jim Bridger	60s	D
	Little Women	Laurie	20s - 30s	S
		Professor Bhaer	Late 30s - early 40s	
1890s	*Dracula*	Van Helsing	Mid 40s - early 60s	D
		Harker	Late 20s - early 40s	
1891	*Paul Bunyan and the Hard Winter*	Rip Snortin' Sam	Late 20s - early 50s	C

Monologues by time period cont.

Year	Play	Character	Age	Tone
1895 to future	*The Time Machine*	Filby	Late 20s - early 40s	D
Late 1800s	*The Adventures of Rikki Tikki Tavi*	Puran Bhagat	Late 60s or older	S
Early 1900s	*Bigger Than Life*	Pecos Bill	Mid 20s - 50s	C
1907	*The Last Leaf*	Old Behrman	73 years old	S
1910	*Pollyanna*	Jimmy Bean	10 years old	S
1912	*Mayfair Lady*	Higgins	40s	S
		Doolittle	40s or older	
1922	*The Great Gatsby*	Nick	30 years old	D
		Gatsby [1]	32 years old	S
		Gatsby [2]		D
1942	*Two Fronts*	Thompson	40s	D
1960s	*A Thing of Beauty*	Jones	20s - 40s	D
1973	*The Swimmer*	Young Man	Late teens	D
Late 1970s	*Lover's Leap*	Reporter	Late 40s - 50s	D
1984	*Playground*	Big John	20 years old	C
2020	*Quaran-Teens*	Josh	16 - 18	S
	Stuck	Unnamed	Teens	D
2021	*The Reunion*	Ali	Late 50s	D
Present	*Alien Invasion!*	Bridger	50s - 60s	C
	Always Bella	Bart	Teens	D
	Amelia, Once More	Alphonse	40s or older	D
		Tom	20s or older	
	Bang! Bang! You're Dead	Actor #3	15 years old	D

Year	Play	Character	Age	Tone
Present	*Bayou*	Tooney	Early teens	C
	The Best Worst Day of My Life	Mr. Ridge	30s - 40s	C
	Black and Blue Friday	Bubba	Teens	C
	A Bowl of Soup	Oscar	Late teens - early 20s	S
	The Boy Who Cried Werewolf	Chris	Early teens	C
	The Boy with No Name	Allen	40s	D
		Eddy	18 years old	
	A Child Went Forth	Boy	Late teens	D
	Cirrius, Nebraska	The Stranger	30s	S
	Disorder in the Court	Scammerton	30s - 40s	C
		Glen	20s - 30s	
	Dr. Evil and the Pigeons with Lasers	Dr. Evil	Late 20s	C
	The Empty Chair	Speaker #5	Teens	D
	Fosters	Petey	Older dog	D
	Gossip	Andy	Teens	D
	If These Walls Could Talk	Stanley	Teens	S
	In the Hood	Guy Jantic	40s or older	C
	Love at First Thought	Norm [1]	Late teens - early 20s	C
		Norm [2]		S
	May I Have Your Attention, Please?	Chris	15 years old	D
	Memory Garden	Dan	Late 30s - early 40s	D
	The Most Viewed Least Watched Talk Show in History	Quinn	20s	C

Monologues by time period cont.

Year	Play	Character	Age	Tone
Present	Rememberin' Stuff	David	Teens	C
		Pete		
		Billy		D
		Tony	18 years old	
	Shakespeare by Monkeys	Riley	20s - 30s	C
	Struggling for the Surface	Joe	40s	D
		James	30s	
	Tested	Will	Teens	D
	The Waiting Room	Robin	50s	D
		Judge	Late 60s - early 80s	
	Walkin' Home	Past George	40s	D
		Stan	20s	
	Why Darkness Seems So Light	Nathan	Teens	D
	Yearbook	Tim	16 - 18	D
Timeless	*The Nose That Ran Away from Its Face*	Nose	Ageless	C
		Boy	Teens	

Appendix C
Monologues by Character Age
◆◆◆

Age	Play	Character	Year	Tone
Ageless	*The Canterbury Tales*	Chanticleer	1300s	C
	Frankenstein	The Creature [1]	1816	D
		The Creature [2]		
	The Nose That Ran Away from Its Face	Nose	Timeless	C
	Sir Huey and the Dragon	Dragon	Once upon a time	C
	The Thirty-Three Little Pigs	Bunker Pig	Once upon a time	C
10 years old	*Pollyanna*	Jimmy Bean	1910	S
Early teens	*Bayou*	Tooney	Present	C
	The Boy Who Cried Werewolf	Chris	Present	C
15 years old	*Bang! Bang! You're Dead*	Actor #3	Present	D
	May I Have Your Attention, Please?	Chris	Present	D
Teens	*Always Bella*	Bart	Present	D
	Black and Blue Friday	Bubba	Present	C
	The Empty Chair	Speaker #5	Present	D
	Gossip	Andy	Present	D
	If These Walls Could Talk	Stanley	Present	S
	The Nose That Ran Away from Its Face	Boy	Timeless	C
	Rememberin' Stuff	David	Present	C
		Pete		
		Billy		D

Monologues by character age cont.

Age	Play	Character	Year	Tone
Teens	*Stuck*	Unnamed	2020	D
	Tested	Will	Present	D
	Why Darkness Seems So Light	Nathan	Present	D
16 years old	*Tuckered*	Prince Willop	Once upon a time	C
16-18	*Quaran-Teens*	Josh	2020	S
	Yearbook	Tim	Present	D
18 years old	*The Boy with No Name*	Eddy	Present	D
	Rememberin' Stuff	Tony	Present	D
Late teens	*A Child Went Forth*	Boy	Present	D
	The Swimmer	Young Man	1973	D
Late teens-early 20s	*A Bowl of Soup*	Oscar	Present	S
	Love at First Thought	Norm [1]	Present	C
		Norm [2]		S
20 years old	*Playground*	Big John	1984	C
20s	*Legend of Sleepy Hollow*	Brom Bones	Early 1800s	S
	The Most Viewed Least Watched Talk Show in History	Quinn	Present	C
	Walkin' Home	Stan	Present	D
20s-30s	*Disorder in the Court*	Glen	Present	C
	Frankenstein	Dr. Victor Frankenstein	1816	D
	Little Women	Laurie	1860s	S
	Pride and Prejudice	Mr. Darcy	Early 1800s	S
	Shakespeare by Monkeys	Riley	Present	C
20s or older	*Amelia, Once More*	Tom	Present	D

Age	Play	Character	Year	Tone
Late 20s	*Dr. Evil and the Pigeons with Lasers*	Dr. Evil	Present	C
Late 20s-early 40s	*Dracula*	Harker	1890s	D
	The Time Machine	Filby	1895 to future	D
20s - 40s	*A Thing of Beauty*	Jones	1960s	D
Mid 20s - 50s	*Bigger Than Life*	Pecos Bill	Early 1900s	C
Late 20s-early 50s	*Paul Bunyan and the Hard Winter*	Rip Snortin' Sam	1891	C
30 years old	*The Great Gatsby*	Nick	1922	D
30s	*Cirrius, Nebraska*	The Stranger	Present	S
30s	*Poe: Dreams of Madness*	Edgar Allan Poe	1840s	D
	Struggling for the Surface	James	Present	D
	The Wall	Gestas	30 AD	D
Mid 30s or older	*The Scarlet Letter*	Arthur Dimmesdale	1700s	D
30s-40s	*The Best Worst Day of My Life*	Mr. Ridge	Present	C
	Disorder in the Court	Scammerton	Present	C
	A Tale of Two Cities	Carton	1790s	D
32 years old	*The Great Gatsby*	Gatsby [1]	1922	S
		Gatsby [2]		D
Late 30s-early 40s	*Little Women*	Professor Bhaer	1860s	S
	Memory Garden	Dan	Present	D
40s	*The Boy with No Name*	Allen	Present	D
	Mayfair Lady	Higgins	1912	S
	Struggling for the Surface	Joe	Present	D
	Two Fronts	Thompson	1942	D
	Walkin' Home	Past George	Present	D

Monologues by character age cont.

Age	Play	Character	Year	Tone
40s or older	*Mayfair Lady*	Doolittle	1912	S
	Scheherazade	Grand Vizier	700 BC	D
Mid 40s-early 60s	*Dracula*	Van Helsing	1890s	D
Late 40s-50s	*Lover's Leap*	Reporter	Late 1970s	D
50s	*The Waiting Room*	Robin	Present	D
50s-60s	*Alien Invasion!*	Bridger	Present	C
Late 50s	*The Reunion*	Ali	2021	D
60s	*Jim Bridger—Mountain Man*	Jim Bridger	1860s	D
Late 60s or older	*The Adventures of Rikki Tikki Tavi*	Puran Bhagat	Late 1800s	S
Late 60s-early 80s	*The Waiting Room*	Judge	Present	D
73 years old	*The Last Leaf*	Old Behrman	1907	S
Older dog	*Fosters*	Petey	Present	D